'Isn't it about time you used your powers for good instead of evil?'

Knowing that she couldn't keep her eyes shut for ever, she took a deep breath and slowly turned around. He was leaning against the stone pillar directly behind her, those dark eyes cool. His lower jaw was covered in golden stubble and his mouth was knifeblade-thin.

That hadn't changed.

A lot else had. She squinted… Tall, blond, built. Broad shoulders, slim hips and long, long legs. He was a big slab of muscled male flesh. When his mouth pulled up ever so slightly at the corners she felt a slow, seductive throb deep in her womb… Oh, dear. Was that *lust?*

Seb stopped in front of her and jammed his hands into the pockets of very nicely fitting jeans.

'Brat.'

His voice rumbled over her, prickling her skin.

Yep, there was the snotty devil she remembered, under that luscious masculine body that looked, and—oh, my—smelled so good. It was in those deep eyes, in the vibration of his voice. The shallow dimple in his right cheek. The grown-up version of the studious, serious boy who had either tolerated, tormented or loathed her at different stages of her life. Always irritating.

'I have a name, Seb.'

He had the audacity to grin at her. 'Yeah, but you know I prefer mine.'

Dear Reader

I write romances about finding love in the twenty-first century, and I love creating quirky heroines—women a little left of centre. Rowan, I think, is one of my quirkiest to date, and she came about when I was watching a travel programme and the female presenter captured my attention. Rowan ran into some minor trouble as a teenager, and as soon as she could left home to travel the world. She's spent years of bouncing from country to country, and I needed to work out what, and who, would make Rowan settle down—especially in her home town, which holds so many bad memories for her.

Seb is Rowan's best friend's brother, her childhood nemesis, and the person whose attention she has always wanted to capture and hang onto. When she finds herself broke and deported, dreading the idea of returning to Cape Town as the family screw-up, it's Seb she reluctantly turns to to help her out of trouble.

As they start discovering the adult versions of the children they used to be they both have to learn to trust, to believe in themselves, in each other and in love itself.

Writing romance is the best job in the world, and I hope you enjoy Seb and Rowan's journey to their happy-ever-after.

With my very best wishes

Joss

xxx

PS Come and say hi via Facebook: Joss Wood, Twitter: @josswoodbooks and Josswoodbooks.wordpress.com

THE LAST GUY
SHE SHOULD CALL

BY
JOSS WOOD

Published in Great Britain 2014
by Mills & Boon, an imprint of Harlequin (UK) Limited,
Eton House, 18-24 Paradise Road, Richmond, Surrey, TW9 1SR

© 2014 Joss Wood

ISBN: 978 0 263 24168 6

Harlequin (UK) Limited's policy is to use papers that are natural,
renewable and recyclable products and made from wood grown in
sustainable forests. The logging and manufacturing processes conform
to the lega...

Printed an...
by CPI A...

Joss Wood wrote her first book at the age of eight and has never really stopped. Her passion for putting letters on a blank screen is matched only by her love of books and travelling—especially to the wild places of Southern Africa—and possibly by her hatred of ironing and making school lunches.

Fuelled by coffee, when she's not writing or being a hands-on mum Joss, with her background in business and marketing, works for a non-profit organisation to promote the local economic development and collective business interests of the area where she resides. Happily and chaotically surrounded by books, family and friends, she lives in Kwa-Zulu Natal, South Africa, with her husband, children and their many pets.

Other Modern Tempted™ titles by Joss Wood:

TOO MUCH OF A GOOD THING
IF YOU CAN'T STAND THE HEAT...

**These and other titles by Joss Wood
are available in eBook format
from www.millsandboon.co.uk**

I love the idea of my characters living happily ever after, but it happens in real life too. My parents and in-laws have been married for 110 years between them. It's a huge achievement and a shining example of the commitment marriage and relationships (in whatever form they might take) require. So this book is dedicated to Frank and Rose and Mel and Elsie for showing us, and our children, how it's done.

CHAPTER ONE

ROWAN DUNN SAT in the hard chair on one side of the white table in an interrogation room at Sydney International Airport and reminded herself to be polite. There was no point in tangling with this little troll of an Immigration Officer; she looked as if she wanted a fight.

'Why have you come to Australia, Miss Dunn?'

As if she hadn't explained her reasons to the Immigration Officer before her—and the one before him. *Patience, Rowan.* 'I bought these netsukes in Bali...'

'These what?'

'A netsuke is a type of miniature carving that originated in the seventeenth century.' She tapped one of the fifteen ivory, wood and bone mini-sculptures that had been stripped of their protective layers of bubble wrap and now stood on the desk between them. Lord, they were beautiful: animals, figures, mythical creatures. All tiny, all perfectly carved and full of movement and character. 'These are uncommon and the owner knew they had value.'

'You bought these little carvings and yet you have no money and no means of income while you are in Australia?'

'That's because I drained my bank account and maxed out my credit cards to buy them. Some of them, I think, are rare. Seventeenth, eighteenth-century. I suspect one may be by Tamakada, circa 1775. I need to get into Sydney to get Grayson Darling, an expert on netsuke, to authenticate them and hopefully buy them from me. Then I'll have plenty of money to stay in your precious, I mean, lovely country.'

'What are they worth?'

Rowan tipped her head. 'Fifteen at an average of two thousand pounds each. So, between twenty and thirty thousand, maybe more.'

The troll's jaw dropped open. 'You've got to be…joking!' She leaned across the table and her face radiated doubt. 'I think you're spinning me a story; you look like every other free-spirited backpacker I've seen.'

Rowan, not for the first time, cursed her long, curly, wild hair and her pretty face, her battered jeans, cropped shirt and well-used backpack. 'I'm a traveller but I am also a trader. It's how I—mostly—make my living. I can show you the deed of sale for the netsuke…'

Officer troll flipped through her passport. 'What else do you sell, Miss Dunn?'

'You've gone through my rucksack with a fine-tooth comb and I've had a body search. You know that I'm clean,' Rowan said wearily. She'd been here for more than six hours—could they move on, please? *Pretty please?*

'What else do you sell, Miss Dunn?'

God! Just answer the question, Rowan, and get this over with. 'Anything I can make a profit on that's *legal*. Art, furniture, antiques. I've flipped statues in Buenos Aires, art in Belize, jewellery in Vancouver. I've worked in construction when times have been lean. Worked as a bar tender when times were leaner. But mostly I buy low and sell high.'

'Then why don't you have a slush fund? A back-up plan? Where is the profit on those deals?'

Fair question.

'A large amount is tied up in a rickety house I've just co-bought with a friend in London. We're in the process of having it renovated so that we can sell it,' Rowan admitted.

And the rest was sitting in those little statues. She knew

that at least one, maybe two, were very valuable. Her gut was screaming that the laughing Buddha statue was a quality item, that it was by a famed Japanese artist. She hadn't planned to wipe out her accounts but the shopkeeper had had a figure fixed in his head and wouldn't be budged. Since she knew that she could flip the netsukes for two or three times the amount she'd paid for them, it had seemed like a short, acceptable risk. Especially since she knew Grayson—knew that he wouldn't quibble over the price. He was the best type of collector: one with deep and heavy pockets. Pockets she couldn't help lighten unless she got into the blinking country!

'The reality is that you do not have enough money on your person to last you two days in Australia.'

'I explained that I have friends...'

The troll held up her hand. 'Your not having enough funds has made us dig a little deeper and we've found out that you overstayed the visa—by six months—on your South African passport.'

Crrr-aa-aa-p!

Rowan felt her stomach sink like concrete shoes. That had happened over eight years ago, which was why she always used her UK passport to get into Oz. She'd been into the country four times since then, but they had finally picked up on her youthful transgression.

Bye-bye to any chance of getting into Oz any time in the next three years. Hello to a very sick bank account for the foreseeable future, to doing the deal with Grayson over the phone—a situation neither of them liked—or to finding another netsuke-mad collector who would pay her well for her gems. There weren't, as she knew, many of them around.

'You are not allowed to visit Australia for the next three years and you will be on the first flight we can find back to South Africa. In a nutshell, you are being deported.'

Rowan looked up at the ceiling and blew a long stream

of air towards the ceiling. It was the only place in the world where she, actively, passionately, didn't want to go. 'Crap.'

The troll almost smiled. 'Indeed.'

Sixteen hours later Rowan cleared Immigration at OR Tambo International in Johannesburg and, after picking up her rucksack, headed for the nearest row of hard benches. Dropping her pack to the floor, she slumped down and stared at her feet.

What now?

Unlike many other cities in the world, she didn't know Johannesburg, didn't have any friends in the city. She had one hundred pounds in cash in her wallet and thirty US dollars. Practically nothing in both her savings and current accounts and her credit cards were maxed out. All thanks to that little out-of-the-way antique shop in Denpasar...

Stupid, stupid, stupid, she berated herself. What had she been thinking? She'd been thinking that she'd triple her money when she flipped them.

'Hey.'

Rowan looked up and saw a young girl, barely in her twenties, take the seat next to her.

'Do you mind if I sit here for a bit? I'm being hassled by a jerk in that group over there.'

Rowan cut a glance to a group of young men who were just drunk enough to be obnoxious. One of the pitfalls of travelling alone, she thought. How many times had she sat down next to a family or another single traveller to avoid the groping hands, the come ons and pick-up lines. 'Sure. Take a seat. Coming or going?'

'Just arrived from Sydney. I saw you on the plane; you were a couple of rows ahead of me.'

'Ah.'

'I'm catching the next flight to Durban. You?'

'Haven't the foggiest.' Rowan tried to sound cheerful

but knew that she didn't quite hit the mark. 'I was deported from Oz and I'm broke.'

Bright blue eyes sharpened in interest. 'Seriously? How broke?'

'Seriously broke.' Rowan lifted her heels up onto the seat of the bench and rested her elbows on her knees. '*C'est la vie.*' She looked at her new friend, all fresh-faced and enthusiastic. 'How long have you been travelling for?' she asked.

'Six months. I'm home for a family wedding, then I'm heading off again. You?'

'Nine years. Can I give you some advice…? What's your name?'

'Cat.'

'Cat. No matter what, always have enough money stashed away so that you have options. Always have enough cash to pay for an air ticket out of Dodge, for a couple of nights in a hostel or hotel. Trust me, being broke sucks.'

She'd always lived by that rule, but she'd been seduced by the idea of a quick return. She'd imagined that she'd be broke for a maximum of three days in Sydney and then her bank balance would be nicely inflated.

It sure hadn't worked out that way… Deported, for crying out loud! Deported and penniless! Rowan closed her eyes and wondered if she could possibly be a bigger moron.

'Can I give you a hundred pounds?' Cat asked timidly.

Rowan eyes snapped open. Her wide smile split her face and put a small sparkle back into her onyx-black eyes. 'That's really sweet of you, but no thanks, honey. I do have people I can call. I would just prefer not to.'

Look at her, Rowan thought, *all fresh and idealistic. Naïve.* If she didn't get street-wise quickly the big bad world out there would gobble her up and spit her out. Travelling in Australia was easy: same language, same culture, good transport systems and First World. Most of the world wasn't like that.

'Your folks happy with you backpacking?'

Cat raised a shoulder. 'Yeah, mostly. They have a mild moan when I call home and ask for cash, but they always come through.'

Rowan lifted dark winged eyebrows. Lucky girl. Could her circumstances be any more different from hers, when she'd left home to go on the road? Those six months between being caught in a drug raid at a club with a tiny bag of coke and catching a plane to Thailand had been sheer hell.

Two months after being tossed into jail—and she still hoped the fleas of a thousand camels were making their home in Joe's underpants for slipping the coke into the back pocket of her jeans, the rat-bastard jerk!—she'd been sentenced to four months' community service but, thanks to the fact that at the time she hadn't yet turned eighteen, her juvenile criminal record was still sealed.

Sealed from the general public, but not from her family, who hadn't reacted well. There had been shouting and desperate anger from her father, cold distance from her mother, and her elder brother had been tight-lipped with disapproval. For the rest of that year there had been weekly lectures to keep her on the straight and narrow. From proper jail she'd been placed under house arrest by her parents, and their over-the-top protectiveness had gone into hyperdrive. Her movements had been constantly monitored, and the more they'd lectured and smothered, the stronger her urge to rebel and her resolve to run had become.

She'd tried to explain the circumstances, but only her BFF Callie had realised how much it had hurt to have her story about being framed dismissed as a lie, how much it had stung to see the constant disappointment on everyone's faces. So she'd decided that she might as well be the ultimate party girl rebel—sneaking out, parties, cigarettes, crazy acting out. Anything to live up to the low expectations of her parents—especially her mother—and constantly, constantly planning her escape.

It had come the day after she'd written her final exam to finish her school career. Using cash she'd received from selling the unit trusts her grandmother had bought her every birthday since the day she was born, she'd bought a ticket to Thailand.

Everyone except Callie had been furious, and they'd all expected her to hit the other side, turn tail and run back home. That first year had been tough, lonely, and sometimes downright scary, but she'd survived and then she'd flourished.

And she really didn't want to go home with her tail tucked between her legs now, broke and recently deported.

She didn't want to lose her freedom, to step back into her family's lives, back into her parents' house, returning as the family screw-up. It didn't matter that she was asset-rich and cash-poor. She would still, in their eyes, be irresponsible and silly: no better than the confused, mixed-up child who'd left nine years before.

'So, who are you going to call?' Cat asked, breaking in on her thoughts.

'Well, I've only got two choices. My mobile's battery is dead and all my contact numbers are in my phone. I have two numbers in my head: my parents' home number and my best friend Callie's home number.'

'I vote for the best friend.'

'So would I—except that she doesn't live there any more. Her older brother does, and he doesn't like me very much.'

Cat leaned forward, curious. 'Why not?'

'Ah, well. Seb and I have always rubbed each other up the wrong way. He's conservative and studious; I'm wild and rebellious. He's mega-rich and I'm currently financially challenged—'

'What does he do?' Cat asked.

Rowan fiddled with her gold hoop earrings. 'His family have a shed-load of property in Cape Town and he oversees that. He also does something complicated with computers. He has a company that does...um...internet security? He's a nice hat... No, that doesn't sound right.'

Cat sat up suddenly. 'Do you mean a white hat? A hacker?'

Rowan cocked her finger at her. 'That's it. Apparently he's one of the best in the world.'

'Holy mackerel...that is so cool! I'm a bit of a comp geek myself.'

'So is he. He's a complete nerd and we've always clashed. He's book-smart and I'm street-smart. His and Callie's house is within spitting distance of my parents' house and I spent more time there than I did at home. I gave him such a hard time.'

Cat looked intrigued. 'Why?'

'Probably because I could never get a reaction out of him. He'd just look at me, shake his head, tell me I was a brat and flip me off. The more I misbehaved, the more he ignored me.' Rowan wound a black curl around her index finger.

'Sounds to me like you were craving his attention.'

'Honey, I craved *everyone's* attention,' Rowan replied.

This was one of the things she loved most about travelling, she thought. Random conversations with strangers who didn't know her from Adam.

'Anyway, I could bore you to death, recounting all the arguments I had with Seb.' Rowan smiled. 'So let this be a lesson to you, Cat. Remember, always have a stash of cash. Do as I say and not as I do.'

'Good luck,' Cat called as she walked towards the bank of public phones against the far wall.

Rowan lifted her hand in acknowledgement. She sure as hell was going to need it.

* * *

Seb Hollis shot up in bed and punched the comforter and the sheets away, unable to bare the constricting fabric against his heated skin. He was conscious of the remnants of a bad dream floating around the periphery of his memory, and as much as he tried to pretend otherwise it wasn't the cool air colliding with the sweat on his chest and spine that made him shiver. The blame for that could be laid squarely at the door of this now familiar nocturnal visitor. He'd been dreaming the same dream for six days… He was being choked, restrained, hog-tied…yanked up to the altar and forced into marriage.

Balls, was his first thought, closely followed by, *Thank God it was only a dream.*

Draping one forearm across his bended knees, Seb ran a hand behind his neck. He was sweating like a geyser and his mouth was as dry as the Kalahari Desert. Cursing, he fumbled for the glass of water on the bedside table, grimacing at the handprint his sweat made on the deep black comforter.

Habit had him turning his head, expecting to see his lover's head on the other pillow. Relief pumped through him when he remembered that Jenna had left for a year-long contract in Dubai and that he was officially single again. He didn't have to explain the nightmare, see her hurt face when he wouldn't talk about the soaked sheets or his pumping breath. Like most women, and despite her corporate career, Jenna had a need to nurture.

He'd never been nurtured and he had no need to be fussed over. It wasn't who he was, what he needed.

Besides, discussing his dreams—emotions, thoughts, desires—would be amusing in the same way an electric shock to his gonads would be nice. Not going to happen. *Ever.*

Intimacy hadn't been part of the deal with Jenna.

Intimacy would never be part of the deal with anyone.

Seb swung his legs off the side of the large bed, reached for the pair of running shorts on the chair next to the bed and yanked them on. He walked over to the French doors that opened onto the balcony. Pushing them open, he sucked in the briny air of the late summer, early autumn air. Tinges of the new morning peeked through the trees that bordered the side and back edges of his property: Awelfor.

He could live anywhere in the world, but he loved living a stone's throw from Cape Town, loved living at the tip of the continent in a place nestled between the mountains and the sea. In the distance, behind those great rolling waves that characterised this part of the west coast, the massive green-grey icy Atlantic lay: sulky, turbulent, volatile. Or maybe he was just projecting his crappy mood on the still sleepy sea.

Jenna. Was *she* what his crazy dreams were about? Was he dreaming about commitment because he'd been so relieved to wave her goodbye? To get out of a relationship that he'd known was going nowhere but she had hoped was? He'd told her, as often and as nicely as he could, that he wouldn't commit, but he knew that she'd hoped he'd change his mind, really hoped that he'd ask her to stay in the country.

It hadn't seemed to matter that they'd agreed to a no-strings affair, that she'd said she understood when he'd explained that he didn't do love and commitment.

Women. *Sheez.* Sometimes they just heard what they wanted to hear.

Seb cocked his head when the early-morning silence was shattered by the distinctive deep-throated roar of a Jag turning into the driveway to Awelfor. *Here we go again,* he thought. The engine was cut, a car door slammed and within minutes he saw his father walking the path to the cottage that stood to the left of the main house.

It was small consolation that he wasn't the only Hollis

man with woman troubles. At least his were only in his head. *Single again,* he reminded himself. Bonus.

'Another one bites the dust?' he called, and his father snapped his head up.

Patch Hollis dropped his leather bag to the path and slapped his hands on his hips.

'When am I going to learn?'

'Beats me.' Seb rested his forearms on the balcony rail. 'What's the problem with this one?'

'She wants a baby,' Patch said, miserable. 'I'm sixty years old; why would I want a child now?'

'She's twenty-eight, dude. Of course she's going to want a kid. Have you told her you've had a vasectomy?'

Patch gestured to the bag. 'Hence the reason I'm back in the cottage. She went bat-crap ballistic.'

'Uh…why do you always leave? It's your house and you're not married.' Seb narrowed his eyes as a horrible thought occurred to him. 'You didn't slink off and marry her, did you?'

Patch didn't meet his eyes. 'No, but it was close.'

Seb rubbed his hand over his hair, which he kept short to keep the curls under control, and muttered an expletive.

'Don't swear at me. You had your own little gold-digger you nearly married,' Patch shot back, and Seb acknowledged the hit.

He'd been blindsided when he'd raised the issue of marriage contracts and his fiancée Bronwyn wouldn't consider signing a pre-nup. Like most things he did, he'd approached the problem of the marriage contracts intellectually, rationally. *He* had the company and the house and the cash, and pretty much everything of monetary value, so *he'd* be the one to hand over half of everything if they divorced.

Bronwyn had not seen his point of view. If he *loved* her, she'd screamed, he'd share everything with her. He *had* loved Bronwyn—sorta…kinda—but not enough to risk sharing his company with her or paying her out for half the value of the house that had been in his family for four generations in the event of a divorce.

They'd both dug their heels in and the break-up had been bruising.

It had taken him a couple of years, many hours with a whisky bottle and a shattered heart until he'd—mostly—worked it all out. He believed in thinking through problems—including personal failures—in order to come to a better understanding of the cause and effect.

It was highly probable that he'd fallen for Bronwyn because she was, on the surface, similar in behaviour and personality to his mother. A hippy child who flitted from job to job, town to town. A supposed free spirit whom he'd wanted—no, *needed* to tame. Since his mother had left some time around his twelfth birthday to go backpacking round the world, and had yet to come home, he'd given up hope that he'd ever get her love or approval, that she'd return and stay put. He'd thought that if he could get Bronwyn to settle down, to commit to him, then maybe it would fill the hole his mother had left.

Yeah, right.

But he'd learnt a couple of lessons from his FUBAR engagement. Unlike his jobs—internet security expert and overseeing the Hollis Property Group—he couldn't analyse, measure or categorise relationships and emotions, and he sure didn't understand women. As a result he now preferred to conduct his relationships at an emotional distance. An at-a-distance relationship—sex and little conversation—held no risk of confusion and pain and didn't demand much from him. He'd forged his emotional armour when his mum had left so very long ago and strengthened it after his experience with Bronwyn. He liked it that way. There was no chance of his heart being tossed into a liquidiser.

His father, Peter Pan that he was, just kept it simple:

blonde, long-legged and big boobs. Mattress skills were a prerequisite; intelligence wasn't.

'So, can I move back in until she moves out?' Patch asked.

'Dad, Awelfor is a Hollis house; legally it's still yours. But I should warn you that Yasmeen is on holiday; she's been gone for nearly a week and I've already eaten the good stuff she left.'

Patch looked wounded. 'So no blueberry muffins for breakfast?'

'Best you're going to get is coffee. No laundry or bed-making service either,' Seb replied.

Patch looked bereft and Seb knew that it had nothing to do with his level of comfort and everything to do with the absence of their elderly family confidant, their moral compass and their staunchest supporter. Yasmeen was more than their housekeeper, she *was* Awelfor.

'Yas being gone sucks.' Patch yawned. 'I'm going back to bed, Miranda has a voice like a foghorn and I was up all night being blasted by it.'

Seb turned his head at the sound of his ringing landline. 'Crazy morning. Father rocking up at the crack of dawn, phone ringing before six…and all I want is a cup of coffee.'

Patch grinned up at him. 'I just want my house back.'

Seb returned his smile. 'Then kick her whiny ass out of yours.'

Patch shuddered. 'I'll just move in here until she calms down.'

His father, Seb thought as he turned away to walk back into the house, was totally allergic to confrontation.

'Seb, it's Rowan…Rowan Dunn.'

He'd recognised her voice the moment he'd heard her speak his name, but because his synapses had stopped firing he'd lost the ability to formulate any words. *Rowan? What the...?*

'Seb? Sorry, did I wake you?'

'Rowan, this is a surprise.' And by surprise I mean... *wow.*

'I'm in Johannesburg—at the airport.'

Since this was Rowan, he passed curious and went straight to resigned. 'What's happened?'

He would have had to be intellectually challenged to miss the bite in the words that followed.

'Why do you automatically assume the worst?'

'Because something major must have happened to bring you back to the country you hate, where the family you've hardly interacted with in years lives and for you to call *me*, who you once described as a boil on the ass of humanity.'

He waited through the tense silence.

'I'm temporarily broke and homeless. And I've just been deported from Oz,' she finally—very reluctantly—admitted.

And there it was.

'Are you in trouble?' He kept his voice neutral and hoped that she was now adult enough to realise that it was a fair question. For a long time before she'd left trouble had been Rowan's middle name. Heck, her first name.

'No, I'm good. They just picked up that I overstayed on my visa years and years ago and they kicked me out.'

Compared to some of the things she'd done, this was a minor infringement. Seb walked to his walk-in closet, took a pair of jeans from a hanger and yanked them on. He placed his fist on his forehead and stared down at the old wood flooring.

'Seb, are you there?'

'Yep.'

'Do you know where my parents are? I did try them but they aren't answering their phone.'

'They went to London and rented out the house while they were gone to some visiting researchers from Beijing. They are due back in…' Seb tried to remember. 'Two—three—weeks' time.'

'You've got to be kidding me! My parents went overseas and the world didn't stop turning? How is that possible?'

'That surprised me, too,' Seb admitted.

'And is Callie still on that buying trip?'

'Yep.'

Another long silence. 'In that case…tag—you're it. I need a favour.'

From him? He looked at his watch and was surprised to find that it was still ticking. Why hadn't time stood still? He'd presumed it would—along with nuns being found ice skating in hell—since Rowan was asking for *his* help.

'I thought you'd rather drip hot wax in your eye than ever ask me for anything again.'

'Can you blame me? You could've just bailed me out of jail, jerk-face.'

And…hello, there it was: the tone of voice that had irritated him throughout his youth and into his twenties. Cool, mocking…nails-on-a-chalkboard irritating.

'Your parents didn't want me to—they were trying to teach you a lesson. And might I point out that calling me names is not a good way to induce me to do anything for you, Rowan?'

Seb heard her mutter a swear word and he grinned. Oh, he did like having her at his mercy.

'What do you want, Brat?'

Brat—his childhood name for her. Callie, so blonde, had called her Black Beauty, or BB for short, on account of her jet-black hair and eyes teamed with creamy white skin. She'd been a knockout, looks-wise, since the day she'd been born. Pity she had the personality of a rabid honey badger.

Brat suited her a lot better, and had the added bonus of annoying the hell out of her.

'When is Callie due back?'

He knew why she was asking: she'd rather eat nails than accept help from *him*. Since his sister travelled extensively as a buyer for a fashion store, her being in the country was not always guaranteed. 'End of the month.'

Another curse.

'And Peter—your brother—is still in Bahrain,' Seb added, his tone super pointed as he reached for a shirt and pulled it off its hanger.

'I know that. I'm not completely estranged from my family!' Rowan rose to take the bait. 'But I didn't know that my folks were planning a trip. They never go anywhere.'

'They made the decision to go quite quickly.' Seb walked back into his bedroom and stared at the black and white sketches of desert scenes above his rumpled bed. 'So, now that you definitely know that I'm all you've got, do you want to tell me what the problem is?'

She sucked in a deep breath. 'I need to get back to London and I was wondering whether you'd loan…'

When pigs flew!

'No. I'm not lending you money.'

'Then buy me a ticket…'

'Ah, let me think about that for a sec? Mmm…no, I won't buy you a ticket to London either.'

'You are such a sadistic jerk.'

'But I *will* pay for a ticket for you to get your bony butt back home to Cape Town.'

Frustration cracked over the line as he listened to the background noise of the airport. 'Seb, I can't.'

Hello? Rowan sounding contrite and beaten…? He'd thought he'd never live to see the day. He didn't attempt to snap the top button of his jeans; it required too much processing power. Rowan was home and calling him. And sounding reasonable. Good God.

He knew it wouldn't last—knew that within ten minutes of being in each other's company they'd want to kill each other. They were oil and water, sun and snow, fire and ice.

Seb instinctively looked towards the window and saw his calm, ordered, structured life mischievously flipping him off before waving goodbye and belting out of the window.

Free spirits…why was he plagued with them?

'Make a decision, B.'

She ignored his shortening of the name he'd called her growing up. A sure sign that she was running out of energy to argue.

'My mobile is dead, I have about a hundred pounds to my name and I don't know anyone in Johannesburg. Guess I'm going to get my butt on a plane ho…to Cape Town.'

'Good. Hang on a sec.' Seb walked over to the laptop that stood on a desk in the corner of his room and tapped the keyboard, pulling up flights. He scanned the screen.

'First flight I can get you on comes in at six tonight. Your ticket will be at the SAA counter. I'll meet you in the airport bar,' Seb told her.

'Seb?'

'Yeah?'

'That last fight we had about Bronwyn…'

It took him a moment to work out what she was talking about, to remember her stupid, childish gesture from nearly a decade ago.

'The one where you presumed to tell me how and what to do with my life?'

'Well, I *was* going to apologise—'

'That would be a first.'

'But you can shove it! And you, as you well know, have told *me* what to do my entire life! I might have voiced some comments about your girlfriend, but I didn't leave a mate to rot in jail,' Rowan countered, her voice heating again.

'We were never mates, and it was a weekend—not a lifetime! And you bloody well deserved it.'

'It was still mean and...'

Seb rolled his eyes and made a noise that he hoped sounded like a bad connection. 'Sorry, you're breaking up...'

'We're on a landline, you dipstick!' Rowan shouted above the noise he was making.

Smart girl, he thought as he slammed the handset back into its cradle. She'd always been smart, he remembered. And feisty.

It seemed that calling her Brat was still appropriate. Some things simply never changed.

CHAPTER TWO

SIX HOURS LATER and it was another airport, another set of officials, another city and she was beyond exhausted. Sweaty, grumpy and… Damn it. Rowan pushed her fist into her sternum. She was nervous.

Scared spitless.

It could be worse, she told herself as she slid onto a stool in the busy bar, her luggage at her feet. She could be standing at Arrivals flicking over faces and looking for her parents. She could easily admit that Seb was the lesser of two evils—that she'd been relieved when her parents hadn't answered her call, that she wasn't remotely sure of their reaction to her coming home.

Apart from the occasional grumble about her lack of education they'd never expressed any wish for her to return to the family fold. They might—and she stressed *might*—be vaguely excited to see her again, but within a day they'd look at her with exasperation, deeply puzzled by the choices she'd made and the lifestyle she'd chosen.

'So different from her sibling,' her mother would mutter. *'Always flying too close to the sun. Our changeling child, our rebel, always trying to break out and away.'*

Maybe if they hadn't wrapped her in cotton wool and smothered her in a blanket of protectiveness she'd be more…normal, Rowan thought. A little more open to putting down roots, to having relationships that lasted longer than a season, furniture that she owned rather than temporarily used.

She'd caused them a lot of grief, she admitted. She'd been a colicky baby, a hell-on-wheels toddler, and then she'd contracted meningitis at four and been in ICU for two weeks, fighting for her life. After the meningitis her family had been so scared for her, so terrified that something bad would happen to her—again—that they hadn't let her experience life at all. All three of them—parents and her much older brother—had hovered over her: her own phalanx of attack helicopters, constantly scanning the environment for trouble.

The weird thing was that while she'd always felt protected she hadn't always felt cherished. Would her life have taken a different turn if she had felt treasured, loved, not on the outside looking in?

It hadn't helped that she'd been a fiery personality born into a family of quiet, brilliant, introverts. Two professors— one in music, the other in theoretical science—and her brother had a PhD in electrical engineering. She'd skipped university in order to go travelling—an unforgivable sin in the Dunn household.

The over-protectiveness had been tedious at ten, irritating at fourteen, frustrating at sixteen. At seventeen it had become intolerable, and by the time she was nearly eighteen she'd been kicking and screaming against the silken threads of parental paranoia that had kept her prisoner.

After spending that weekend in jail she'd realised that to save herself and her relationship with her family she had to run far away as fast as she could. She couldn't be the tame, studious, quiet daughter they needed her to be, and they couldn't accept her strong-willed adventurous spirit.

Running away had, strangely enough, saved her relationship with her parents. Through e-mail, social media and rare, quick phone calls they'd managed to find a balance that worked for them. They could pretend that she wasn't gallivanting around the world, and she could pretend that they supported her quest to do more, see more, experience more.

They all lied to themselves, but it was easier that way.

Now she was back, and they couldn't lie and she couldn't pretend. They had to see each other as they now were—not the way they wished they could be. It was going to suck like rotten lemons.

Rowan hauled in a deep breath… She had two, maybe three weeks to wrap her head around seeing her parents, to gird herself against their inevitable disappointment. Two weeks to find a place to stay and a job that would keep her in cereal and coffee and earn her enough money to tide her over until she sold her netsukes.

She just had to get past Seb—whom she'd never been able to talk her away around, through or over. He'd never responded to her charm, had seen through her lies, and had never trusted her for a second.

He'd always been far too smart for his own good.

The image of Seb as she'd last seen him popped into her head. Navy eyes the colour of deep denim, really tall, curly blond hair that he grew long and pulled back into a bushy tail with a leather thong, and that ultra-stupid soul patch.

Yet he'd still turned female heads. Something about him had always caught their attention. It was not only his good looks—and, while she wished otherwise, she had to admit that even at his most geeky he *was* a good-looking SOB—he had that I-prefer-my-own-company vibe that had woman salivating.

Live next door to him and see how you like him then, Rowan had always wanted to yell. *He's bossy and rude, patronising and supercilious, and frequently makes me want to poke him with a stick.*

Rowan draped her leg over her knee and turned her head

at deep-throated male laughter. Behind her a group of guys stood in a rough circle and she caught the eye of the best-looking of the bunch, who radiated confidence.

Mmm. Cute.

'Hey,' Good-looking said, in full flirt mode. 'New in town?'

I'm tired, sweaty, grumpy and I suspect that I may be way too old for you.

'Sort of.'

Good-looking looked from her to the waiter standing next to him. 'Can I buy you a drink? What would you like?'

A hundred pounds would be useful, Rowan thought. *Two hundred would be better...*

'Thanks. A glass of white wine? Anything dry,' she responded. Why not? If he wanted to buy her a drink, she could live with it. Besides, she badly needed the restorative powers of fermented grape juice.

He turned, placed the order with the waiter, and when Rowan looked again she saw that he wasn't quite so young, not quite so cocky. Tall, dark and handsome. And, since she was bored waiting for Seb, she might as well have a quick flirt. Nothing picked a girl up and out of the doldrums quicker than a little conversation with a man with appreciation in his eyes.

She thought flirting was a fine way to pass the time...

Rowan pushed a hand through her hair and looked at the luggage at their feet. 'Sports tour? Hmm, let me guess... rugby?' Rowan pointed to the bags on the floor with their identical logos. 'Under twenty-one rugby sevens tournament?'

'Ah... They are under twenty-one...I'm not.'

Rowan smiled slowly. 'Me neither. I'm Rowan.'

She was about to put her hand out for him to shake when a voice spoke from behind her.

'Isn't it about time you used your powers for good instead of evil?'

Rowan closed her eyes as the words, words not fit to speak aloud, jumped into her head. Knowing that she couldn't keep her eyes shut for ever, she took a deep breath and slowly turned around.

He was leaning against the stone pillar directly behind her, those dark blue eyes cool. His lower jaw was covered in golden stubble and his mouth was knife-blade-thin.

That hadn't changed.

A lot else had. She squinted... Tall, blond, built. Broad shoulders, slim hips and long, long legs. He was a big slab of muscled male flesh. When his mouth pulled up ever so slightly at the corners she felt a slow, seductive throb deep in her womb... Oh, dear. Was that lust? It couldn't be lust. That was crazy. It had just been a long trip, and she hadn't eaten much, and she was feeling a little light-headed... It was life catching up with her.

Mr Good-looking was quickly forgotten as she looked at Seb. She'd known a lot of good-looking men, and some devastatingly handsome men, but pure lust had never affected her before... Was that why her blood was chasing her heart around her body? Where had the saliva in her mouth disappeared to? And—oh, dear—why was her heart now between her legs and pulsing madly?

Rowan pushed a long curl out of her eyes and, unable to meet his eyes just yet, stared at his broad chest. Her gaze travelled down his faded jeans to his expensive trainers. Pathetic creature to get hot and flustered over someone she'd never even liked.

Hoo, boy. Was that a hint of ink she saw on the bicep of his right arm under his T-shirt? No way! Conservative Seb? Geeky Seb?

Except that geeky Seb had been replaced by hunky Seb, who made her think of cool sheets and hot male skin under her hands... This Seb made her think of passion-filled nights and naughty afternoon sex. Of lust, heat and attraction.

Thoughts at the speed of light dashed through her head as she looked for an explanation for her extreme reaction. She was obviously orgasm-deprived, she decided. She hadn't had sex for....oh, way too long. Right! If that was the problem—and she was sure it was—there was, she remembered, a very discreet little shop close to home that could take care of it.

Except that she was broke... Rowan scowled at her shoes. Broke and horny...what a miserable combination. Yet it was the only explanation that made a smidgeon of sense.

Seb stopped in front of her and jammed his hands into the pockets of very nicely fitting jeans.

'Brat.'

His voice rumbled over her, prickling her skin.

Yep, there was the snotty devil she remembered. Under that luscious masculine body that looked and—oh, my—smelled so good. It was in those deep eyes, in the vibration of his voice. The shallow dimple in his right cheek. The grown-up version of the studious, serious boy who had either tolerated, tormented or loathed her at different stages of her life. Always irritating.

'I have a name, Seb.'

He had the audacity to grin at her. 'Yeah, but you know I prefer mine.' He looked over at Mr Good-looking and his smile was shark-sharp. 'Lucky escape for you, bro'. She's trouble written in six-foot neon.'

As rugby-boy turned away with a disappointed sigh, inside his head Seb placed his hands on his thighs and pulled in deep, cleansing, calming breaths of pure oxygen. He felt as if his heart wanted to bungee-jump from his chest without a cord. His stomach and spleen were going along for the ride.

Well, wasn't *this* a kick in the head?

This was *Rowan*? What had happened to the skinny kid with a silver ring through her brow and a stud in her nose? The clothes that she had called 'boho chic' but which had looked as if she'd been shopping in Tramp's Alley? Skirts that had been little more than strips of cloth around her hips, knee-high combat boots, Goth make-up...

Now leather boots peeked out from under the hem of nicely fitting blue jeans. She wore a plain white button-down shirt with the bottom buttons open to show a broad leather belt, and a funky leather and blue bead necklace lay between the wilted collar of the shirt. Her hair was still the blue-black of a starling's wing, tumbling in natural curls down her back, and her eyes, black as the deepest African night, were faintly shadowed in blue. Her face was free of make-up and those incredible eyes—framed by dark lashes and brows—brimmed with an emotion he couldn't immediately identify.

Resignation? Trepidation and fear? Then she tossed her head and he saw pride flash in her eyes.

And there was the Rowan he remembered. He dismissed the feeling that his life was about to be impacted by this tiny dark-haired sprite with amazing eyes and a wide, mobile mouth that begged to be kissed.

He'd said goodbye to a kid, but this Rowan was all woman. A woman, if she were anyone but Rowan, he would be thinking about getting into bed. Immediately. As in grabbing her hand, finding the closest room and throwing her onto the bed, chair, floor...whatever was closer.

His inner cave man was thumping his chest. *Look here, honey! I'm a sex god!* He felt embarrassed on his own behalf. *Get a grip, dude!*

He hoped his face was devoid of all expression, but in his mind Seb tipped his head back and directed a stream of silent curses at the universe. *When I asked what else could*

*go wrong, I meant it as a figure of speech—not as a chal-
lenge to hit me with your best shot.*

Rowan broke the uncomfortable silence. 'So…it's been a long time. You look…good.'

'You too.'

Good? Try sensational!

'Where did you fly in from?' he asked. Politeness? Good grief, they'd never been civil and he wondered how long it would last.

'Sydney. Nightmare flight, I had a screaming baby behind me and an ADD toddler in front of me. And the man in the seat next to me sniffed the entire time.'

'Two words. Business class.'

Rowan grimaced. 'One word. Broke.'

She shoved a hand into her hair, lifted and pushed a couple of loose curls off her face.

'Would you consider changing your mind about loaning me the money to get back to London?'

Rowan threw her demand into the silence between them.

Thirty seconds from polite to miffed. It had to be a record.

'Well? Will you?'

*Sure—after I've sorted out climate change and negoti-
ated world peace.* 'Not a chance.'

Rowan tapped an irritated finger on the table and tried to stare him down. Seb folded his arms and kept his face blank.

Eventually her shoulders dropped in defeat. 'My mobile battery is dead, I have less than two hundred pounds to my name, my best friend is out of the country, my parents are away and their house is occupied. I'm in your hands.'

In his hands? He wished… Their eyes met and sexual attraction arced between them. Hot, hard… *Man!* Where was this coming from?

Pink stained Rowan's cheekbones. 'I mean, I'm at your mercy...'

That sounded even better.

'What is the matter with me?'

Or at least that was what he thought he heard her say, but since she was muttering to the floor he couldn't be sure.

What was cranking their sexual buzzers to a howl? *Dial it down, dude; time to start acting as an adult.* He dashed the rest of what was left in the tiny bottle of wine into her glass and tossed it back.

Think with your big head. It didn't matter that she looked hot, or that he wanted to taste that very sexy mouth, this was Rowan. AKA trouble.

Seb put his hands into the back pockets of his jeans. 'You ready to go?'

'Where to? Where am I sleeping tonight?'

'Awelfor.'

Awelfor... It meant sea breeze in Welsh, and was one of the few small holdings situated between the seaside villages of Scarborough and Misty Cliffs, practically on the doorstep of Table Mountain National Park. Her second home, Rowan thought.

The house had originally been an old school building, added to over the generations. The oldest part was made from timber and redbrick, and she could still feel the cool warmth of the Oregon pine floors beneath her bare feet. Nearly every room had a fireplace and a view of the Atlantic, with its huge rolling waves and its white beaches peppered by black-backed gulls.

She'd been raised next door, in the house that had been built by a Hollis forefather for—rumour had it—a favourite mistress. It had been sold off in the forties to her grandfather and separated from the Hollis house by a huge oak and a high, thick Eugenia hedge.

She knew Awelfor as well as she knew her own home:

which floorboard creaked if you stood on it the middle of the night, that the drainpipe that ran past Callie's window was strong enough to hold their combined weight, that Yasmeen the housekeeper hid her cigarettes in the flour canister at the back of the pantry. For most of her life she'd had two homes and then she'd had none; now she bounced from bed to bed in different accommodation establishments, depending on her cash flow. Once or twice she'd slept on beaches and on benches in railway stations, she remembered, even standing up.

Dots appeared behind her eyes.

Tired...so tired.

Rowan blinked furiously as the dots grew bigger and brighter and her vision started to blur. She reached out in Seb's direction and cool and firm fingers clasped her clammy hand.

'What's the matter?' Seb demanded as she abruptly sat down again. .

'Dizzy,' Rowan muttered as she shoved her head between her knees. 'Stood up too fast.'

Rowan opened her eyes and the floor rose and fell, so she closed them again.

'Easy, Ro.'

Seb bent down in front of her and held up three fingers. 'How many?'

'Six thousand and fifty-two.'

Seb narrowed his eyes and Rowan gnawed the inside of her lip, ignored the squirming sensation down below and tried to act like a mature adult.

'Sorry, I'm fine. Tired. I haven't really eaten properly. Shouldn't have had that wine.' Rowan rubbed her eyes. 'It's just been a horrible couple of days.'

Seb let go of the hand he'd been holding and stood up, looking away from those slim thighs in old jeans, that mad hair and those deep, deep eyes. She had always been gorgeous—hadn't all his friends told him that?—but for the first time in his life he saw her as something other than his sister's friend.

That felt uncomfortable and…weird.

His eyes dropped lower. Full breasts under that white cotton shirt, long fingers that were made to stroke a man's skin, long legs that could wrap around a man's hips…

This was *Rowan*, he reminded himself harshly. She was not somebody he should find attractive. He'd known her for far too long and far too well. Seb frowned, irritated that he couldn't break their eye contact. Her eyes had the impact of a fist slamming into his stomach. Those eyes— the marvellous deep dark of midnight—had amused, irritated and enthralled him. When he'd first met her he'd been a young, typical boy, and babies were deeply uncool but her eyes had captivated him. He remembered thinking they were the only redeeming feature of a demanding, squawking sprat.

Her face was thinner, her bottom rounder and her hair longer—halfway down her back. He imagined winding those curls around his fingers as he slipped inside her… Seb shook his head. They shared far too many memories, he reminded himself, a whole handful of which were bad, and they didn't like each other much.

Have you totally lost your mind?

'Let's get you home and we can argue later, when you're back to full strength.' Seb bent down and easily lifted her rucksack with one hand, picking up her large leather tote with the other. 'You okay to walk?'

Rowan stood up and pulled her bag over her shoulder. 'Sure.'

Seb briefly closed his eyes. It was a struggle not to drop her bags and bring her mouth to his.

'What's the problem now?' Rowan demanded, her tone pure acid.

He stared at the ceiling before dropping rueful eyes back to her face. 'I keep thinking that it would've been easier if you'd just stayed away.'

'Loan me the cash and I'm out of here,' she pleaded.

'I could…'

Rowan held her breath, but then Seb's eyes turned determined and the muscle in his jaw tightened. 'No. Not this time, Ro. You don't get to run.'

CHAPTER THREE

ROWAN SAT IN the passenger seat of Seb's Audi Quattro SUV as he sped down the motorway towards Cape Town. Although it was a little before eight in the evening, the sun was only just starting to drop in the sky and the motorway was buzzing with taxi drivers weaving between cars with inches to spare and shooting out the other side with toothy grins and mobiles slapped against ears.

Cape Town traffic was murder, no matter what the time of day. It came from having a freaking big mountain in the middle of the city, Seb thought. He glanced at his watch; they'd been travelling for fifteen minutes and neither of them had initiated conversation. They had another half-hour until they reached Awelfor and the silence was oppressive.

Seb braked and cursed as the traffic slowed and then came to a dead stop. Just what he needed. A traffic jam and more time in the car *not* speaking to each other. At the best of times he wasn't good at small talk, and it seemed stupid, and superfluous to try to discuss the weather or books, movies and music with Rowan.

And on that point, since it was the first time that Rowan had been in the same time zone as her parents for nearly a decade, he felt he owed it to them to keep her in the country until they got a chance to see her, hold her. Like him, they didn't wear their hearts on their sleeves, but he knew that they had to miss her, had to want her to come back. He could sympathise. He knew what it felt like, waiting for a loved one to come home.

He had never been able to understand why she didn't value her family more, why she rebelled so much. She had parents who took their jobs seriously; he and Callie had a runaway fickle mother and…Patch. As charming and entertaining as Patch was, he was more friend than father.

Rowan's parents, Heidi and Stan, had always been a solid adult presence right next door. Conservative, sure, but reliable. Intelligent, serious, responsible. On a totally different wavelength from their crazy daughter. Then again, it sounded as if Rowan operated on a completely different wavelength to most people, and he had enough curiosity to wonder what made her tick.

Since this traffic was going nowhere they had time to kill and nothing else to talk about, so he would take the opportunity to satisfy his nosiness.

He and Ro had never danced around each other, so he jumped straight in.

'I want to know why you're broke. I know that you consider yourself a free spirit, too cool to gather material possessions, but surely a woman your age should have more to her name than a hundred pounds?'

She'd known this was coming—had been bracing herself for the lecture. Because Cape Town was synonymous, in her mind, with being preached to.

Rowan pursed her lips as she looked straight ahead. Seb hadn't lost his ability to cut straight through the waffle to what he thought was important. Lord, she was too tired to tangle with that overly smart brain of his. Too weirded out by the fact that he made her ovaries want to dance the tango. What to say without sounding like a complete idiot?

Keep it simple, stupid.

'I was doing a deal and I was supposed to get paid for delivering the…the order when I got into Oz.'

'What were you peddling, Rowan?'

Seb's eyes turned to dark ice and his face hardened when she didn't answer. Of course he couldn't take that statement at face value. He needed more and naturally he assumed the worst. She knew what he was thinking...

Here we go again, Rowan thought, *back where I started.* As the memories rolled back her palms started to sweat and she felt her breath hitch. Even after so many years Seb still instinctively assumed the worst-case scenario. As her parents would... And they wondered why she hadn't wanted to come home.

'It wasn't anything illegal, Seb!'

'I never said it was.'

'I'm not an idiot or a criminal! And, while I might be unconventional, I'm not stupid. I do not traffic, carry or use drugs.' Rowan raised her voice in an effort to get him to understand.

'Calm down, Ro. For the record, back then I never believed you should have been arrested,' Seb stated, and his words finally sank in.

Rowan frowned at him as his words tumbled around her brain. 'You didn't? Why not?'

'Because while you were spoilt and vain and shallow—and you made some very bad decisions—you were never stupid.'

She couldn't argue with that—and why did it feel so good that Seb believed she was better than the way she was portrayed? Just another thing that didn't make any sense today.

But she knew that Seb's opinion was one that her parents wouldn't share.

'But, Rowan, this lifestyle of yours is crazy. You're an adult. You should not be getting kicked out of countries. You should have more than a backpack to your name. Most women your age have established a career, are considering marriage and babies…'

Shoot me now, Rowan thought. *Or shove a hot stick in my eye.* This was why she hadn't wanted to come home, why she didn't want to face the judgment of her family, friends and whatever Seb was. They'd always seen what they wanted to see and, like Seb, wouldn't question the assumption that she was terminally broke and irreversibly irresponsible.

Rowan's eyes sparked like lightning through a midnight sky. 'What a stupid thing to say! You don't know anything about me!'

'And whose fault is that? You were the one who ran out of here like your head was on fire!'

'I didn't run!' Okay, that lie sounded hollow even to her.

'Within days of writing your finals you were on a plane out of the country. You didn't discuss your plans with anybody. That's running—fast and hard.' Seb's finger tapped the steering wheel as the car rolled forward. 'What really happened that night?'

Rowan lifted her chin. 'I don't know what you mean.' He couldn't know, could he? Callie might have told him… No, she'd sworn that she wouldn't, and Callie would never, ever break her word. Seb had to be talking about her life in general and not that night she'd got arrested in particular.

That stupid, crazy, change-her-life evening, when she'd fallen from heaven to hell in a few short hours.

'Sure you do.' Seb scanned the road ahead, saw that the traffic wasn't moving and sighed. 'Something in you changed that night you were arrested… You were rebellious before, but you were never spiteful or malicious or super-sarcastic.'

Her attitude had been that of a rabid dog. In the space of one night she'd gone from being wildly in love and indescribably happy to being heartbroken, disparaged and disbelieved. That night *had* changed her life. After all, not everybody could say that they'd lost their virginity, got dumped and framed by their lover, then arrested all in the same night. And her weekend in jail had been a nightmare of epic proportions.

Was it any wonder that she equated love with the bars of a jail?

'You were never that hard before, Rowan.' Seb quietly interrupted her thoughts. 'Those last six months you fought constantly with your parents, with me, with the world.'

Rowan clenched her jaw together. Every night she'd cried herself to sleep, sick, heartsore, humiliated, and every day she'd got up to fight—literally—another day.

'Maybe I was crying because my parents, my sibling and everyone close to me left me to spend the weekend in jail when they could've bailed me out any time during the day on Friday. The party was on a Thursday night.'

'Your parents wanted to teach you a lesson,' Seb replied, his voice steady.

Rowan stared at the electronic boards above his head. 'Yeah, well, I learnt it. I learnt that I can only rely on myself, trust myself.'

When she dared to look at him again she saw that his eyes were now glinting with suppressed sympathy. Then amusement crept across his face. 'Yet here you are relying on me.'

'Well, all good things have to come to an end,' Rowan snapped back.

She was so done with being interrogated, and it had been a long time since she'd taken this amount of crap from anyone.

'So...' She smiled sweetly. 'Hooked up with any gold-diggers lately?'

Annoyance replaced sympathy in the blink of an eye. 'Sending me those sunglasses when you heard that we'd split was a very unnecessary gesture,' he said through gritted teeth.

'I know, but I thought you might need them since you finally saw the light. It took you long enough.'

'Very droll.' Seb's hands tightened on the steering wheel.

'Still annoyed that flighty, fey Rowan pegged your ex's true characteristics and you didn't?' Rowan mocked, happy to shift the focus of their conversation to him.

'Remind me again as to why I didn't leave you to beg in Jo'burg?'

'You wanted to torture me. So, are we done biting each other?'

'For now.'

As the traffic began to move Rowan watched Seb weave his way through the slower-moving vehicles to speed down the fast lane.

'Has the traffic got worse?' she asked when Seb slammed on his brakes and ducked around a truck. Her hand shot out and slammed against the dashboard. The last vestiges of colour drained from her face. 'Sebastian! Dammit, you lunatic!'

Seb flipped her a glance and then returned his attention to the road, his right hand loosely draped over the steering wheel. 'What's the problem?'

'The problem is that you missed the bumper of that car by inches!' Rowan retorted, dropping her hand. 'The traffic hasn't got worse—your driving has!'

Seb grinned. 'Don't you think it's a bit early in our relationship to start nagging?'

'Bite me.'

Seb flipped the indicator up and made a production of checking his side and rearview mirrors. He gestured to a sedan in front of him. 'Okay, brace yourself. I'm going to overtake now. Here we go.'

Rowan sighed and rolled her eyes. 'You are such a moron.'

Seb ducked around another sedan, and flew across two lanes of traffic to take the exit. Rowan leaned back in her seat, closed her eyes and thought it was ironic that she'd crossed seven lanes of motorbikes in Beijing, a solid stream of tuk-tuks in Bangalore and horrific traffic in Mexico to die in a luxury car in her home country at the hands of a crazy person.

Rowan sat up and looked around as they drove into a more upscale neighbourhood and she recognised where she was. 'Nearly ho... there.'

'Yep, nearly *home*. And, despite your inability to say the word, this *is* still your home, Ro.'

'It hasn't been my home for a third of my life,' Rowan corrected, thinking that she had a twitchy heart, a spirit that was restless, a need to keep moving. Coming back to Cape Town broke made her feel panicky, scared, not in charge of her own destiny. She felt panic well up in her throat and her vocal cords tighten.

Seb's broad hand squeezing her knee had her sucking in air. When she felt she had enough to breathe she looked at his hand and raised her eyebrows. Then she pulled her eyebrows closer together when she clocked the gleam in his eyes, the obvious glint of masculine appreciation.

'You've grown up well, Brat.'

Bemused by the sexual heat simmering between them, she tried to take refuge in being prosaic. 'I haven't grown at all. I'm the same size I was at eighteen—and don't call me Brat. And take your hand off my knee.'

The corners of his eyes crinkled. 'It worked to take your mind off whatever you were panicking about. You always did prefer being angry to being scared.'

Seb snorted a laugh when she picked up his hand and dropped it back onto the gearstick.

'Have you developed any other serious delusions while I've been away?'

'At eighteen…' Seb carried on talking in that lazy voice that lifted the hair on her arms '…you wore ugly make-up, awful clothes and you were off the scale off-limits.'

Rowan, because she didn't even want to attempt to work out what he meant by that comment, bared her teeth at him. 'I'm still off-limits.'

Seb ignored that comment. 'Is that why you are still single at twenty-eight…nine… What? How old *are* you?'

'Old enough to say that my relationship status has nothing to do with you.'

'*Relationship status?* What are you? A promo person for Facebook?' Seb grimaced. 'You're either married, involved, gay or single. Pick one.'

Rowan snorted her indignation. 'Gay? For your information, I like what men have. I just frequently don't like what it is attached to!'

'So—single, then?'

'I'd forgotten what an enormous pain in the ass you could be, but it's all coming back.' Rowan turned and tucked herself into the corner between the door and seat. At least sparring with Seb was keeping her awake. 'And you? Any more close calls with Satan's Skanks?'

She hoped the subject of his ex-fiancée would be enough of a mood-killer to get him off the subject of her non-existent love-life.

'You really didn't like her.' Seb twisted his lips. 'Was it a general dislike or something more specific?'

There wouldn't be any harm in telling him now, Rowan thought. 'She was seriously mean to Callie. I mean, off the scale malicious.'

Seb's eyes narrowed. 'I thought they got along well.'

'That's what she wanted you to think. She was a nasty

piece of work,' Rowan said, staring at the bank of dials on the dashboard. 'I really didn't like her.'

'I would never have guessed,' Seb said dryly.

'My "money-grabbing" comment didn't clue you in?'

'It was a bit restrained.' Seb's tone was equally sarcastic. 'Your efforts to sabotage our engagement party were a bit subtle too.'

'What did I do?' she demanded, thinking that attack was the best form of defence. 'And why would I do it since I was looking forward to you being miserable for the rest of your life?'

Seb slid her an ironic glance. 'Apart from spiking the punch with rum? And turning the pool that violent green that totally clashed with the puke-orange colour scheme? And placing a condom on every side plate? Anything I've missed?'

Rowan dropped her head back on the headrest. 'You knew about that?'

'I had a good idea it was you.' Seb's lips twitched. 'Okay, hit me. What else did you do?'

'Nothing,' Rowan replied, far too quickly.

'Come on, 'fess up.'

Well, he couldn't kill her now. She didn't think…

'I put itching powder in your bed.'

Rowan felt as if she wanted to dance to the sound of Seb's laughter. Despite her now overwhelming fatigue, she noticed the scar bisecting his eyebrow, the length of his blond eyelashes. Man, she wanted to link her arms around him, curl up against him and drift off.

'Ro, I knew about that too.'

He spoke softly and Rowan felt both warm and chilled, her nerve-endings on fire.

'Luckily we had a fight after the party and I chose to sleep in the spare room…she itched for days.'

'Good.' Rowan grinned and fought an enormous yawn. 'You had really bad taste in women, Seb.'

'She wasn't so bad. And if I didn't know any better I'd say you sound like a jealous shrew.'

'You really should give up whatever you're smoking.'

Rowan lifted her nose. As if she'd be jealous of that waste of a womb. Seb might be a thorn in her side but he was *her* thorn in the side—and Callie's, obviously. Nobody else was allowed to treat him badly. Especially not some lazy, stupid... Oh, dear God, the old oak tree was still on the corner of their road.

And there, through the trees, she could see the redbrick corner of Awelfor.

'No, don't panic. Just breathe. It's only a house, Ro.'

His house. And next door was her old home. And a life she didn't want to go back to—a life she'd outgrown a long time ago.

Seb turned into his driveway and parked in front of a new rectangular automated gate. While he waited for the gate to slide open he looked at Rowan, his blue eyes serious. 'Stay the three weeks, spend some time with your parents, and then I'll loan you the money to fly anywhere in the world.'

'Why?'

'Because I think it's long overdue.'

Rowan shook her head, suspicious. 'How much time, exactly, must I spend with them?'

Seb looked frustrated. 'I don't know! Make an effort to see them—have dinner with them—talk to them and we'll have a deal.'

It was too good an offer to pass up. It wasn't ideal but it was a solid plan of action. If she got some money together before that she'd go sooner... No, she couldn't do that. She was here. She had to see them. To leave without saying hello would be cruel, and she wasn't by nature cruel. Three weeks. What was twenty-one days in the scheme of things?

Twenty days too long in this city, her sarcastic twin said from her shoulder.

'I'll pay you back.'

Seb grinned. 'Yeah, you will. Yasmeen is on holiday and we're short of a housekeeper. You can start tomorrow: shopping, cleaning, laundry, cooking. You know what Yas does.'

'Are you mad? I'm not going to housekeep for you!' Rowan protested.

It wasn't that she couldn't—she'd worked as a maid before—but she wasn't going to pick up after Seb and his 'we'.

'We're? You said *we're* short of a housekeeper? Who else lives here?' Rowan demanded. If he had a live in lover/partner/girlfriend then she'd just go and sleep on the beach.

Seb steered the car up to his elegant house. 'Patch has hit a hiccup with his current girlfriend and has moved back into the second floor of the cottage.'

Oh, thank goodness. She didn't know if she could cope with Seb and any 'significant other'.

'So, housekeeping in exchange for your bed and food?'

'S'pose,' Rowan reluctantly agreed, thinking that she was jumping from the frying pan into... Well, the third level of the hot place.

After lugging Rowan's luggage up to Callie's old bedroom Seb finally made it to his office—the bottom floor of the two-bedroomed cottage Patch had moved into—temporarily he hoped! His workaholic staff worked flexible hours, so he was accustomed to seeing them at work at odd times, and Carl, his assistant/admin manager, like his hackers, was still around.

Seb listened to Carl's update and accompanied him into what they called the 'War Room'. The huge room was windowless, and a massive plasma TV attached to the far wall was tuned to MTV at a volume level that made his ears bleed. He picked up the TV remote that stood in its cradle on the wall and muted the volume. Two male heads and one female head shot up and looked in his direction.

His hackers needed junk food, tons of coffee and music. Deprive them of one of the three and he had their immediate attention. Seb walked into the centre of the room and rapidly scanned the long row of screens where computer code rolled in an unending stream. He read it as easily as he did English, and nodded when he didn't immediately pick up any problems.

'Anything I should know about?' he asked, folding his arms.

He listened while they updated him on their individual projects—testing the security of a government agency, a bank and a massive online bookseller—adding his input when he felt he needed to but mostly just listening while they ran their ideas past him. There was a reason why he'd hired all three and paid them a king's ransom: they were ethical, super-smart and the best in the field.

Nearly, but not quite, as good as him.

Seb wrapped up the meeting, left the room and headed for his office, which was diametrically opposite to the War Room. There were computers—five of them—with a processing power that could run most Developing World countries—but his office had lots of natural light, a TV tuned to ESPN, an *en-suite* bathroom and a door directly linked to the gym. Although he nagged and threatened, his staff members rarely used the up-to-date equipment.

Seb tossed his car keys and mobile onto his desk, hooked his chair with his foot and pulled it over to his favourite computer. Having Rowan return with her battered backpack and her world-weary attitude made him think of his mother and had him wondering where she was laying her head these days. He checked on her once or twice a year—

with his skills he could find out exactly where she was, how much money she had and pretty much what she was up to. He'd first tracked her down when he was sixteen and he'd found her passport and identity number on a supposedly coded list—ha-ha!—on his father's computer.

His fingers flew across the screen as he pulled up the program he'd written specifically to let him track her. Within minutes he found out that she'd drifted from Peru to Brazil and then moved around a bit within that country. She was currently in Salvador and running seriously low on funds.

He experienced the usual wave of resentment and anger, wondered if he was a hundred types of a fool—after all, what had she ever done for him?—and then transferred a thousand untraceable dollars into her account. It was less than petty cash to him, and if he didn't do it he'd lie awake at night, wondering what she'd have to do to dig herself out of that hole. She was, after all, his mother.

Rowan was in pretty much the same position, he thought, and he wondered how she'd come to the same point. He looked at his screen speculatively and thought that with a couple of clicks he could find out exactly what had happened to bring her home. He had everything he needed: her passport number, her bank details. He could, by inputting a line of code into that program, see her travel movements and everything she'd ever purchased with a credit or debit card.

It was that easy.

He'd done it before—not for five years at least, but once or twice a year before that, when her parents hadn't heard from her for a while and her father had asked him to take a peek. He'd skim over the information, not particularly interested, and report back that she was in London or Perth and reassure them that she seemed to have enough money to cover her costs. There were big deposits and big withdrawals, but there was always a savings account with excess funds. He wondered why she hadn't had one this time…

Seb dropped his hands to his lap and fought temptation. He could, but he didn't—as curious as he was, he didn't have the right to invade her privacy. She wasn't the child they had all worried about anymore, she'd grown up.

She was now the knockout she'd promised to be. Eyes the colour of night, wild hair, creamy, creamy skin and a body that was all woman. He felt his zipper straining and leaned back in his chair, spun around and stared out of the window to the pool area beyond his floor-to-ceiling windows. He wanted her. And, equally and as intensely, he didn't want to want her. She was everything he avoided in the opposite sex: complicated, gregarious, communicative…free-spirited and forthright.

Why hadn't he just loaned her the money and sent her on her way? Then he wouldn't be sitting here—being totally unproductive—with an urge to see if she slept naked.

He was such a moron.

'Gray, I'm really sorry…'

Seb propped his shoulder against the doorframe to his newly refurbished kitchen, with its sleek cupboards, black granite and black and white checked floor. Yasmeen had designed the kitchen and, since this was where she ruled from, he'd been happy to write out the rather hefty cheque. It was filled with light, modern appliances and Yasmeen's precious ferns and African Violets. If he let those die his life would be over.

He grinned. It was just another job he could add to Rowan's growing list of housekeeping duties.

'Grayson…take a breath. There's a monkey, a tiger with cubs, a squid, a seal and a horse. Those are the highlights. And a Hotei.'

What on earth was she up to? Seb wondered as he stepped into the kitchen and headed for the coffee machine.

'I'm pretty sure the Hotei is rare. It has that…class, a mastery that just can't be ignored.'

Rowan nodded when he lifted a cup towards her, asking whether she wanted coffee.

'Now that my mobile is charged again I'm about to e-mail you some photographs. Take a look and see what you think… Yes, I know that you won't buy anything without looking at it…'

Rowan murmured a couple of soothing phrases into the mobile before disconnecting the call. She quickly e-mailed Grayson the photographs she'd promised and placed her mobile onto the kitchen table.

'I *know* that you can't buy them without seeing them. I've only been dealing with you for ten years. Jerk.'

Seb handed her a cup of coffee which Rowan reached for with the enthusiasm of a true coffee addict.

'Thanks. You need a master's degree to operate your machine.'

Seb leaned against his counter and thought that Rowan looked a great deal better than she had when he'd picked her up. That was what a solid night's sleep did for you, Seb thought. She still had faint blue shadows under her eyes, but there was at least some colour in her cheeks. He'd checked on her a couple of times and discovered that she didn't—unfortunately—sleep naked, that she had a slight piggy snore and that she slept on her stomach.

'Are you trying to sell a zoo?' Seb said, his eyes on her long legs. She wore a simple pair of denim shorts and another button-down cotton shirt and had pulled her clean hair into a fat plait. She wore no make-up except for a slick of gloss on her lips.

She took his breath right away.

'Of sorts. I picked up some stuff in Bali which I hoped to flog when I got to Oz.'

And he'd thought that *he* was tight-lipped and uncommunicative. It made him want to shake her...or kiss her. 'You know I *could* just avoid pulling your teeth for information and find out for myself.'

'How?'

He wiggled his hands. 'Magic computer fingers.'

'Corny. And, like most men, I think you exaggerate your computer skills.' Her expression was a mixture of pity and disbelief, as if he was a child telling tall stories.

'Sweetheart, I hacked into the FBI's website and left them an Easter egg when I was sixteen—'

'A what?'

'An Easter egg. It's a surprise in a program that a hacker leaves...a signature or a message or a picture. It's non-malicious. Anyway, if I wanted to I could tell you what you had for breakfast six years ago, so finding out what you bought in Bali would be child's play.'

Rowan's look threatened to cut him off at the knees. 'If I find out that you've done that—ever—I will make it my personal mission to make your life on earth resemble the hottest part of hell.'

Seb knew that that she'd certainly try. And he'd watch her try for a while and then he'd get bored and haul her off to bed... Actually, that didn't sound like a bad plan at all. Entertainment in and out of the bedroom. Win-win.

'*Have* you ever done that?'

'Cyber checked up on you?' Seb slid his innocent expression into place—the one he'd been practising since he was fourteen and had discovered code and that he could speak it. And have some fun with it. 'Why would you think that?'

'Because I don't trust you further than I can throw you. Have you?'

Of course he had. She'd been nineteen, on her own in

countries where she couldn't speak or read the language. Her parents had been beside themselves with worry—actually, her father had. Her brother Peter had been concerned. Callie a little less so. Himself? Not so much... He'd always known that Rowan was stronger, smarter than they gave her credit for. He'd known that she'd be fine but he'd used his skills to check up on her so that the family and friends she'd left behind could sleep at night.

'Have you?'

He was saved from answering that question by her chirping mobile, which rattled and vibrated on the dining room table as if it was possessed. Rowan narrowed her eyes at him—a non-verbal threat that he wasn't off the hook—and frowned when she looked down at the tiny screen.

'Grayson...again?'

Rowan yanked the mobile up to her ear as her heart bounded up her throat. There was no reason for Grayson to be returning her call so soon unless she'd found the netsuke of the century or there was a huge problem.

It turned out to be both. Rowan listened to his garbled words and tried to make sense of what he was saying. 'Are you saying that my netsukes might have been stolen? From a West End art gallery a year ago?'

Rowan rested her forehead on her hand and tried to force the panic far away enough so that she could listen to Grayson.

'A seal, a stag antler, a tiger with cubs and a squid were stolen from the King and Cross Gallery. There's been a lot of interest in netsuke lately, and consequently a lot of theft. They are also easy to transport, being not much bigger than the size of a golfball.'

'If they were stolen, how did they end up in a hole-in-the-wall shop in Bali? They were covered in dust, forgotten. Nobody had looked at them for years.'

'I can't take a chance that these might be stolen. Didn't you get any provenance?'

'Gray, the guy said they were pawned. The owner never came back to pick them up and that was six years ago.' Rowan rubbed her neck. 'They are *not* stolen.'

Grayson was silent for a minute. 'Well, if these are genuine eighteenth-century netsuke and aren't the same objects that were stolen then I think you've got a heck of a find on your hands.'

'So, it's either really good or really bad news?'

'Essentially. Can you prove how you paid for them?' Grayson demanded.

Rowan's eyes flicked to Seb's face. He was listening to her side of the conversation with avid interest.

'Yeah. Every cent. I drained my bank accounts to pay for them.'

'That's good. Of course you might take a financial hit if they *are* stolen, but if you can prove you paid for them then it shows you didn't have criminal intent.'

'Yay me. And they *aren't* stolen.' Rowan closed her eyes at the thought of waving goodbye to twelve thousand pounds. She rested her forehead on the dining room table and tried not to hyperventilate.

'Of course if they are not stolen, then I think you've hit a massive pay-day,' Grayson added.

Rowan heard Seb move from his chair and thought that he was finally giving her some privacy. Instead she felt his hand warm and big on her neck, gently stroking the tense cords.

She wished she could just lean back and soak up his strength, ask him to help her sort this out. But she couldn't. She never asked for help...mostly because there had never been anyone around she could ask.

Besides, he'd just think that she was stupid and

irresponsible… And because she liked his hands on her skin a little too much she swatted them away.

'Do you have any documentation or photographs of what was stolen from that gallery so that I can compare them myself?' Rowan asked Grayson.

'No, that's not my problem—it's yours. I just know that it was those four subjects.'

And Japanese artists never did the same subjects. Damn Grayson! He was getting all paranoid and crazy without even knowing if the netsukes looked the same. Stupid man. Grayson was rich, but he wasn't bright.

'You need to do some research. Try to identify the pieces. Then we'll talk again,' Grayson said as Seb dropped his hand and walked away to refill his coffee cup.

'You know you want them.'

'And I'll buy them—after you tell me that they are definitely not stolen.'

'They are definitely not stolen.'

'Smarty pants,' Grayson said, before disconnecting.

Aurrrrgh. It wasn't as if she was a total amateur, Rowan thought on an internal eye-roll. She stared out of the window and tried to push her way through her panic to think the problem through.

'I can smell your brains burning,' Seb said, taking his seat again and pushing another cup of coffee in her direction. 'Sip and spill.'

Rowan instinctively shook her head. 'Don't worry about it. I'll figure something out.' She pushed against the table to haul herself to her feet. This wasn't Seb's problem, she thought. It was hers, solely.

Rowan looked down in surprise when Seb's hand snagged her wrist and tugged her back to her seat. 'Sit down, drink your coffee and tell me what's happened.'

'Seb…I can deal with it. It's fine.'

Seb shoved a frustrated hand through his hair. 'That's

the problem, Rowan. You don't need to deal with it on your own. Why won't you let me help you?'

'I don't need your help! This is minor, Seb. I *needed* your help nine years ago. I needed lots of help then! Since then I've learnt to rely on myself.'

Seb flicked his thumbnail against his bottom lip. 'Something happened that night—something more than any of us realised.'

Rowan shook her head. 'What is your obsession with that damned party? It was at a club, I got caught with a baggie, I did community service for it… End of story.'

'Really? I suspect you took the rap for that slick character you were so in love with. Jason… Jack…' Seb clicked his fingers in frustration.

'Joe Clark.'

He frowned. 'The same Joe Clark who runs that sports betting company? The one that's just been listed on the Stock Exchange?'

'I presume so. His father owned a couple of betting shops, so it must be the same family.'

'You haven't kept in touch with him?'

Revulsion passed across Rowan's face, accompanied by a visible shudder. Oh, yeah, there was a story here.

Rowan cocked her head. 'What's with the twenty questions? I feel like I'm back in the interrogation room at Sydney.'

'You're tough. You can handle it.' Seb looked over the rim of his coffee cup. Her remote, distant façade was back in place and it annoyed him. She wasn't cool and remote. She never had been. Loud, vivacious, spontaneous… He'd used to be able to read every emotion on her face.

'Are you in trouble—again?' If she was there was no way that he'd just sit back and watch her go through hell a second time. 'Tell me.'

Rowan recognised that determined look on his face and

realised that he wasn't going to be shrugged off. And she felt…relieved. Glad to have an excuse to tell him, to tell somebody.

Another part of her wanted to show him—tell him that she *wasn't* the ditsy, silly, crazy child who bounced from job to job, wafting her way through the world. Well, she did waft, but she worked as well. Being an art 'picker' took determination, time and a good eye. And hours and hours of studying jewellery, art, sculpture.

Maybe he could respect that—respect her?

Was it so wrong to want a little affirmation, a little admiration from a super-smart man? From anybody?

'Criminal trouble? No. Financial trouble? Oh, yeah. And to make you understand I have to show you something,' Rowan said, and walked out of the room to fetch her baby sculptures.

CHAPTER FOUR

'I LOVE THIS one,' Seb said, holding the chubby, joyful figurine of a Buddha in the palm of his hand. 'Simply stunning.'

'It's a Hotei, also called a Laughing Buddha, symbolising contentment and abundance and luck.' Rowan's finger drifted over the Buddha's cheek. 'I love him too. I think he's the prize of the collection.'

After Seb had spent at least fifteen minutes looking at the tiny ivory netsukes, pointing out details that she hadn't noticed, Rowan rewrapped the carvings and put them back into their box. Closing the lid, she wrapped her hands around her coffee cup. She wondered where to start. At the beginning, she supposed…

'After six months in Thailand I left and headed for Hong Kong, I had a job teaching English and was barely scraping by. One day, after I'd just been paid, I was on my way to buy groceries, and there was a little shop I passed every day, full of…curiosities, I suppose. Mostly junk, to be honest. I had some time and I went in. I was browsing through a box of costume jewellery and I found a brooch. I knew right away that it was special. The craftsmanship was superb. The owners thought it was paste but I knew it wasn't. Don't ask me how. I just did.'

Seb leaned his arms on the table, listening intently.

'I went straight to the Causeway District and found an antique shop.'

Seb's mouth kicked up in a smile. 'Don't tell me… It was solid gold and studded with diamonds.'

'Better. It was Fabergé and worth a freaking fortune. I was lucky. The owner paid me a fair price. He could've ripped me off. I didn't know what it was. The profit on that funded my travels for the next eighteen months, but I was hooked on the chase. I started studying antiques, jewellery, art. I realised I had an eye for spotting quality and, while I never found another Fabergé brooch, I *did* find Lalique glassware, Meissen pottery, minor works of art. I made some money.'

Well, that explained the deposits and withdrawals. Smart girl, Seb thought. Smart *and* gorgeous. A very dangerous combination.

'Most of my capital is tied up in a house I co-bought in London which I am planning on…'

'Flipping?'

Rowan tipped her mouth up. 'It's what I do.'

'So, coming back to these…'

Rowan told him what Grayson had said and waited through his resultant thoughtful silence. 'So, basically, you need to know whether these are previously undiscovered, undocumented netsuke or whether they've been stolen?'

'They aren't stolen. I'm pretty sure of that. But no one is going to buy them at the price I want without further information.' Rowan rested her chin on her fist. 'And obviously it also means that I'm going to be broke for a lot longer than I anticipated.'

Seb waved her money troubles away. Easy for him to do, Rowan thought.

'So, what's the next step?' he asked.

'Research. Lots of it. I don't know nearly enough about netsuke.'

'But you know that they are quality pieces? Do you need my computer skills?'

'I don't think so… I just need to trawl through databases of documented netsuke and see if I can find any of them.'

'Well, if you need to get into places that you can't get into…'

'Is that what you do? Poke around in places?'

Seb shrugged. 'At a very basic level.'

'What exactly are you paid so much money to do?'

Seb tapped his finger against his coffee cup. 'I guess you can call me a consultant. Companies hire me to evaluate their computer systems for vulnerabilities. So I go in there, try to hack their system—and pretty much always do. Then I point out where they have problems. Sometimes I fix the problems for them; sometimes they get their people to do it. Either way I get paid.'

'Huh. So you use your powers for good and not evil?' Rowan threw his words back at him.

'Yeah.'

'And you'd be willing to…poke around for me? Isn't that illegal?'

'Slightly unethical, maybe.' Seb's eyes were determined when they met hers. 'Look, I'm not going to use the information for personal gain, and if it helps you out of a jam then so much the better.'

Rowan nodded her understanding, thought for a minute, then said, 'Let me do some research. If I need your help, I'll ask.'

'Promise?' Seb shrugged at her gimlet stare. 'It's just that you don't have a great track record when it comes to asking for help, Brat.'

'Promise. Can I borrow a computer?'

'Sure. There's a couple you can use in my office, or there's a few you can use in my bedroom.' Seb deliberately wiggled his eyebrows suggestively and Rowan, as expected, rolled her eyes. Yep, time to bust her chops, he thought, and to banish the tension he saw in her eyes.

'I am not going anywhere near your bedroom, Hollis.'

Seb leaned back in his chair. 'Why? Scared you won't be able to keep your hands off me?'

'What? Are you mad? You're like my...my...er...'

'Don't say brother,' Seb ground out. 'That would be too creepy for words.'

'No...geez! *Eeuuuw!*' Rowan shuddered as she banged her cup onto the table. 'No talk of bedrooms!'

Seb liked the colour in her face and the snap in her eyes so he thought he'd wind her up some more. 'Okay, can we talk about what happens in bedrooms, then?'

'We could *never* have sex!'

'Uh, yes...actually we could. You see, my Part A would slot into your Plot B—'

Rowan's look was meant to freeze. 'Stop being facetious! It's a crazy idea! Yes, I think you've got some heat happening, but it would be a really stupid thing to do. We don't even like each other.'

Seb stood up and ran a hand over her head. Then he placed one hand on the back of her chair and bent down so that his face was next to hers. She just folded her arms and lifted a perfectly arched, perfectly arrogant eyebrow. *Man,* that look made him hot.

'Are you trying to intimidate me? It didn't work when I was ten—what makes you think it'll work now?'

'I was just wondering whether you taste as good as you smell.'

'You'll never find out.' Rowan pushed him away, stood up and put some distance between them. She placed her fists on her hips and tipped her head. 'Back to business. So, if I ask you for help what is it going to cost me?'

'What?'

'Your computer skills? I'm already paying for my food and bed by being the housekeeper...'

Seb looked at the stack of dishes in the sink. 'Not that you've done any housekeeping yet.'

'Give me a break. I'll get to it! So, what's the price?'

'We'll work something out,' Seb said, deliberately vague.

'And that statement scares the hell out of me,' Rowan retorted. 'As per usual you've managed to drive me crazy, so I need to leave. I'm going to do some shopping, since there isn't anything to eat in this house!'

'Want me to come with you?'

'I've been shopping on my own for a long time now. I think I can manage.'

Rowan made her tone even and unemotional, but Seb smiled at the twin strips of colour on her cheekbones. Her chest was flushed and her nipples were puckered against her shirt. Her mind and mouth might be protesting at the thought of them sleeping together but her body wouldn't object. He could reach for her right now and he knew that she wouldn't take much persuading…

Except that he wanted her to want this—him—with both her body and mind. He didn't want her to have regrets, to think that she was coerced. That would be giving that smart mouth of hers too much ammunition to chew his ass off.

Rowan wasn't known for playing fair.

'Money.' Rowan held out her hand and bent her fingers backwards and forwards. When he just looked at her, she sighed. 'I can't go shopping without money, Einstein, and I don't have any.'

Right. Try to keep up, Hollis! Seb reached into his back pocket, pulled out his wallet and handed over a wad of bills. He had no idea how much was in there and it didn't matter. Money was easy. She could blow every cent he had and he would just put his shoulder to the wheel and make some more.

People—it was people who baffled him, he thought as Rowan tucked the cash into the pocket of her jeans.

'Keys?' she asked.

'To what?'

'Your car. Or were you expecting me carry the groceries back in the basket on the front of a bicycle?'

'There is no way I'm letting you drive my precious car.' Seb walked over to a row of hooks by the door and lifted off a set of keys. 'Here's a remote to the gate and garage and the keys to Yas's runaround. Use that.'

'I can't use Yasmeen's car!'

'It's my car, and Yas uses it to do errands so that she doesn't risk getting her own dinged.' Seb tossed her the set of keys and Rowan snatched them out of the air.

Their glances clashed and electricity buzzed between them again. Except that this time—dammit—it wasn't all sexual, wasn't only a caveman impulse to score with a pretty girl. Rowan wasn't just a pretty face and a spectacular bod; she'd be easier to resist if she were.

She had a brain behind those amazing eyes, a sharp sense of business and a talent to spot art. Being physically attracted to her was enough of a hassle. To be mentally drawn to her as well was asking for trouble.

Yet he was having to fight to keep from taking those couple of steps to her, pulling her against him and making her his.

Seb placed his fists on his hips and blew out a long, frustrated breath. He needed to think this through, to rationalise this attraction he felt to her. Needed to try to find out where these crazy impulses to get her naked were coming from. He believed in being rational, in analysing that which he didn't understand.

And he didn't understand what was happening with him where Rowan was concerned. He needed to get a handle on these unpredictable and swamping impulses he had whenever she was in the same room.

Like the impulse to strip her naked and bend her over the back of that chair…

Oh, man. He was in a world of trouble here…

'Okay, well, I'll be back later.' Rowan flashed him an uncertain look and belted out through the kitchen door.

Seb gripped the back of a chair with both hands and dropped his head. What was wrong with him? He never went nuts over a woman—never, ever felt out of control. Sex was important and, like all men, he liked it—no, he loved it—but he had always been able to walk away. Always.

Until now. Until Rowan.

And she hadn't even been back in his life for twenty-four hours. She had already tipped his world upside down and Seb shuddered when he thought of the chaos she could create in the immediate future.

He was still so annoying, Rowan thought as she went into the empty, cavernous hall of the supermarket and walked over to the fresh fruit section.

'My Part A would slot into your Plot B—'

Seb's words rattled around her brain. A stupid phrase that had lust whirling in her downstairs regions, that made her feel light-headed—oh, dear, that made her sound like a heroine from a historical romance, but it was the perfect word—and created an impulse to reach up and yank that sardonic mouth to hers.

She'd never felt the impulse to yank—*yank?*—any man's mouth to hers, and that it was Seb's that she now had the urge to taste went against all the laws of the universe.

She could not believe that she—cool, competent and street-smart—was acting like a horny teenager, about to collapse in a panting, wet, drippy, drooling heap at his feet.

It was humiliating. Really!

Rowan pushed a tendril of hair out of her eyes and blew

air into her cheeks as her mobile chirped. Pulling it from the front pocket of her shorts, she did an excited wiggle when she saw the name in the display window.

'Ro? Honey?' The gravelly voice of her best friend boomed across the miles.

'Why aren't you in Cape Town, where I need you?' Rowan demanded. 'The one time I get back and you're not here, Callie!'

'Sorry, darling. I got delayed... He's six-two and has soulful green eyes. And I need to see a designer in LA who can only see me next week. Or maybe the week after.'

'Naff excuse,' Rowan muttered.

'So, how and why are you back home?'

'It's a long story.'

Rowan gave her a brief synopsis of her last couple of days. After thinking about and then refusing Callie's offer of a loan, she sighed into the mobile.

'Something else is wrong,' Callie stated. 'Come on—spit it out.'

'I don't know what you're talking about.'

'In the last fifteen minutes I think you said Seb's name once. Normally you would've insulted him at least ten times by now. What's going on?'

And that was the problem with knowing someone for all your life. You couldn't sneak stuff past them. 'I don't know if you want to know.'

'I always want to know. Spill.'

'I think I suddenly have the screaming hots for my best friend's brother.'

When Callie stopped roaring with laughter Rowan put the mobile back to her ear.

'Holy fishcakes,' Callie said. 'Sweetheart, when you muck it up, you do it properly.'

Rowan frowned at Callie's uncharacteristically mild expletives. 'Holy *fishcakes*? *Muck* it up?'

'My temporary fling nearly had heart failure when I dropped the F-bomb yesterday; he's a bit conservative. I'm cleaning up my potty mouth.'

Rowan laughed and winced at the same time. That would last as long as the fling did: until Callie got on the plane to come home.

'Anyway, tell me about wanting to do my brother.'

Rowan grimaced. *Do* her brother? *Eeew.* Knowing that Callie wasn't going to drop the subject without getting something out of her, she thought about what to say. 'I've never had this reaction to anyone—ever! I just want to take a bite out of him.'

While she wasn't a nun, she'd had some sex over the years. Sporadic, erratic, infrequent, but it had been sex. Two one-night stands, a few season-long relationships, and once a relationship that had lasted a year.

'It's about time you ran into someone who set you on fire. The fact that it's Seb just makes we want to wet my pants with laughter.'

'Glad you find it amusing. I don't. I don't know how to deal with it,' Rowan muttered, leaning her hip against a display stand of orange sweet potatoes. Instead of discussing Seb further, she chose to shove her head in the sand. 'So, tell me about your fling.'

'Hot, conservative, sweet. And you're changing the subject because you don't want to deal with your sexy side!'

'Bye, Cal, love you.'

'Avoiding the issue isn't going to change it—'

'Miss you. Hurry home, okay? I need you!' Rowan interrupted, before disconnecting.

Rowan rolled her shoulders in frustration, thinking about her 'sexy side'. Sex had always just been nice and pleasant. Uncomplicated. It gave her a little buzz. But she could probably live without it if she had to. Just as she could live without having a permanent man in her life, being in a permanent place. She had never given her heart away—couldn't, because she still hadn't learnt not to look at a man and wonder if he she could trust him. She didn't need sex and she definitely didn't need love.

She'd managed without it all these years and probably wouldn't know what to do with it if she found it. And if she occasionally yearned for it then it meant that she was human, didn't it?

She wouldn't mind some respect, though.

She'd loved Joe. Had been passionately, deeply, mind-blazingly in love with him. The type of love you could only experience when you were eighteen and everything was black and white. Somewhere in the part of her that was all woman—mysterious and wise—she'd known that Joe would be the guy who would change her destiny, would alter her mindset, would change her in ways that she'd never believed possible.

She'd never considered that her love for him would spin her life in such a different direction…

Rowan was pulled back from her memories by a store announcement and found herself staring at piles of fruit, multi-coloured vegetables, the perfection of the display.

Apples as red as the poisonous fruit in *Snow White*, atomic orange carrots, purple eggplant. Six different types of lettuce, herbs, sweet potatoes…and no people. At nine in the morning the supermarket was all but deserted.

She looked down and saw the aisles, shelves packed full of consumer goods. Where were the shouts of the vendors in Tamil? The smell of lemongrass and hot oil? So much abundance, so much choice, no people. So much artificial colour, piped music that hurt her ears…no people. Where was everybody? How could there be so much choice and no one to choose?

She wanted to be back in the markets in Hanoi, standing in a queue to touch a statue of Buddha in Phuket, on a crowded train on her way to Goa.

She didn't want to be back here, in the city that held so many bad memories for her. She didn't want to deal with Seb, who set her blood on fire, made her feel things that were hot and uncomfortable. She didn't want to deal with her parents, revisit her past.

She wanted to be back on crowded streets, on the Inca trails in Peru, in an Outback logging town in the Yukon. She wanted to be on her own, having transient relationships with people who expected little or nothing from her.

She wanted her freedom, she thought as she left the supermarket empty-handed. Her independence, solitude.

Money in the bank.

Money... *Dammit,* Rowan thought as she turned around and walked back into the shop. She'd made a deal with the devil and part of that deal required her to shop for food.

Ugh.

After she'd spent a healthy amount of Seb's money Rowan drove towards the coast and onto the main road that led to the beach in the area. Behind her sunglasses her eyes widened with surprise as she took in the changes that had occurred since she'd left. Her favourite beach was still there—of course it was—but the buildings on the other side of the road had been converted into upscale boutiques and gift shops, restaurants and a coffee shop-slash-restaurant-slash-neighbourhood bar.

Rowan headed straight for the restaurant/bar and slid into a tiny table by the window. She ordered an espresso and a slice of cheesecake and silently told herself that she'd add it to the mental tab she owed Seb.

It was such a stunning day. She could see Table Mountain, blue, green and purple, a natural symbol of this incredibly beautiful city. The sea was flat, aqua and green, and the sun glinted off the white sand.

Rowan looked up at the waitress and pointed to the 'Help Wanted' sign on the door. 'I see you need another waitress?'

'A bartender, actually.'

Even better, Rowan thought. She loathed waitressing. 'Tips good?'

'Very. You interested? If you are, I can call the manager over.'

Rowan nodded and within fifteen minutes had agreed to tend bar on Friday night as a trial. If that worked out she could have three night shifts a week. Rowan agreed with alacrity... She'd do anything to add cash to her depleted coffers so she could leave this city as soon as possible.

A stream of feminine cursing distracted Rowan from her appreciation of the scenery and she turned to see a fifty-something fashion plate slip into a chair at the table next to her. She was fantastically turned out, with styled curly hair, large breasts and long legs in skinny jeans. She wore Audrey Hepburn glasses and a very sulky expression. Rowan felt like a garden gnome next to her.

Rowan took a bite of cheesecake and sighed as the flavours burst onto her tongue. The lady gestured a waiter forward and pushed her sunglasses up into her hair. Fine lines surrounded her light green eyes and Rowan revised the estimate of her age upwards. Maybe closer to sixty, but looking good. She pointed to Rowan's cup and cheesecake.

'I think she wants the same,' Rowan told the confused waitress, and smiled when the blonde lifted her thumb.

'What do you mean you've made a mistake?' she shouted into her cell, in a French-accented voice. '*L'imbécile!* I booked the Farmyard on the fourth, and I don't care if you double-booked with the President himself. Unbook it!'

Rowan rested her chin in the palm of her hand and didn't

pretend that she wasn't listening. She was fascinated. What was the Farmyard? A brothel? A nightclub? A restaurant?

'How am I going to explain to my seven-year-old grandson that he can't have his party there? Are *you* going to explain?'

Or a children's party venue.

After swearing very comprehensively, in both English and French, at the Farmyard's representative, she snapped her mobile closed and rested her head on her folded arms.

Rowan felt her sympathy stirring and leaned over and touched her on the arm. 'Hey.'

She might not be able to make emotional connections to places or things but she'd never had a problem talking to anyone, making casual connections that could last a minute, an hour, a day…

The blonde head lifted, the sunglasses slid down the pert nose and Rowan noticed tears in the dark eyes. 'What's the matter? Can I help?'

The woman shoved her glasses up her nose and sniffed. 'Only if you can provide a venue for twenty-five kids in ten days' time, complete with horses and a mini-quadbike track and paintball shooting. And an army tank cake.'

'Pardon?'

'I booked this exclusive children's party venue for next Saturday and they double-booked it. I'm going to have to cancel the party and I am going to break my grand-baby's heart. I'm Annie, by the way.'

'Rowan,' Rowan replied as her mind started to whirl. She knew of a place that had horses, a paddock suitable to make a mini-quadbike track, and haybales to make up a mock battle field for paintball-shooting. 'What's your budget?'

The Jane Fonda look-alike frowned at her and named a figure.

Rowan swallowed and wasn't sure if she'd heard her

properly. Who paid that sort of money for a kid's party? Were these people nuts? He was seven and not the Sultan of Brunei's kid!

Rowan stood up, picked up her plate and moved to the blonde's table. 'My name is Rowan, but my friends call me Ro...let's chat.'

When Seb was twenty-two, Patch had told him that he was handing over the family's property portfolio to Seb to manage and that he was going to open up a company in Simon's Town, doing sea-kayaking tours.

Seb hadn't believed him, but within six months he'd had the added responsibility of managing various warehouses, office blocks and houses around Cape Town, Patch had moved out of Awelfor and into a house in Simon's Town and had started leading tourist tours showing off Signal Hill, Lions Head and Table Mountain from a sea perspective.

The company had taken off, and he'd opened a branch in Hermanus, but most days he still went out on the water and led a tour. For Seb, Patch's Kayak Tours was just across the peninsula, and he often found himself driving to Simon's Town, running along the promenade and joining his dad for an early-evening paddle.

Today it had been easy, paddling in the shelter of the harbour, and he'd soon pulled ahead of the group in the open sea, wanting to feel the strain in his arms and his shoulders. Skirting a navy striker ship waiting to dock, he headed south towards the world-famous Boulders Beach as he kept an eye out for whales. He flew past the huge rocks at Boulders, laughing at the penguin colony that stood on the beach contemplating hunting for food, and after a half-hour turned back and caught up with the sluggish tour.

Seb laughed again as two endangered Black Oyster Catchers pecked at Patch's hat and with a pithy insult drew abreast with him. He cursed when his mobile jangled in its waterproof jacket. He put it to his ear and ignored Patch's hiss of displeasure.

'No mobiles on the water, Sebastian!' Patch said loudly.

Recognising the number at Awelfor, Seb ignored Patch and quickly answered it. 'Rowan, what's wrong?'

'Nothing. Well—um—I need to ask you a favour.'

Rowan's voice sounded hesitant and his face cleared. Oh, this should be good. Another favour? She was racking them up!

'What is it?'

'May I hold a function here on Saturday?'

'I thought you were broke! Do you have money to entertain?'

'It's not entertaining…exactly. I need a place to host a birthday party for some kids and I kind of suggested Awelfor.'

Seb thought that she had to be joking. 'You kind of *what*?'

'This lady will pay me a grotesque amount of money to organise a kid's birthday party and I need a place to make a track for mini-quads and to set up a paintball course.'

Seb dropped his hand, looked at his phone and shook his head. 'Are you nuts? I don't want kids all over my property!'

'You won't even be here! I saw that notice on the fridge for a trail run you're doing on Saturday!' Rowan protested.

'Rowan, you've been in the country two days and you've already managed to meet someone who can give you a job. How is that possible? And how do you know she's not a con?'

'Oh, maybe because she'll pay me sixty per cent of the fee up front,' Rowan whipped back. 'Yes or no, Seb? If it's no I need to go to Plan B.'

'Do you have a Plan B?' Seb asked, curious. Patch leaned over to yank his mobile out of his hand and he jerked away.

'No, but I will have to find one if you say no. Please don't say no.'

'Why do I suspect that you've already told her that you can host the party at Awelfor?'

'Because I have,' Rowan said in a small voice. 'Sorry. But I'll make another plan if you *really* mean no.'

He wasn't even surprised or, come to think of it, that upset. If anyone else took such liberties with his house and his property he'd have a fit of incredible proportions, but Rowan had been such a part of Awelfor for so long that it wasn't that much of an intrusion or an imposition. Weird, but true.

'Okay, knock yourself out. However, when you agree to house a shedload of monkeys, or a circus comprising of Eastern European acrobats, run it by me first, okay? Got to go.' Seb disconnected and shoved his mobile away before Patch could yank it away. He'd lost two mobiles to Patch's strict rule about 'disturbing the peace'.

'I'm going to ban you from joining my tours,' Patch complained.

'Sorry,' Seb replied, and picked up his paddle again and pulled it through the water.

They rowed for a while in companionable silence until Patch spoke again.

'So, what's Ro done this time?' Patch asked.

Seb explained and Patch laughed.

'Life certainly has been less…colourful without her presence.'

'But a great deal more sensible.'

'Sensible…*pshaw*! I had coffee with her this afternoon. It's lovely to have her home,' Patch said. 'I've always loved that girl.'

Seb sent him a measuring look. 'I know you did when she was a kid, but…'

Patch pointed out a seal to his group, exchanged some banter with them and turned back to Seb. 'But?'

'Doesn't she remind you of…Mum?'

Patch was silent for a minute and then shook his head. 'The only commonality between the two is that they both like to travel. No, Seb. Ro is nothing like Laura. Ro would never leave her kids—leave the people she loved and never make contact again.'

'She did for a couple of months,' Seb pointed out.

Why was he pushing this? What did he hope his father would say? *Yes, she's exactly like Laura and that he should run as if his tail was on his fire*? Would that make his big brain override his little one and cancel out all the X-rated visions he was having about her?

Patch's slow, measured words pulled him back into the conversation.

'Everyone seems to have forgotten that Ro sent Callie regular e-mails, asking her to tell Stan and Heidi and us that she was fine. She was a little lost and she was trying to find herself. When she had enough distance from her parents she made contact again. Ro didn't have it easy at home, Sebastian.'

'They loved her, Dad,' Seb protested.

'As much as they could. But she needed so much more. She wouldn't have run if she'd felt loved. They didn't understand her, and sometimes I think that's worse. Don't get me wrong—I like Stan and Heidi—but I think Peter fulfilled all their requirements for a child. Studious, quiet, introverted, brilliant and unemotional. Having to deal with an emotional hurricane like Rowan rocked their world.'

'Maybe. And she *is* an emotional hurricane.' And, because he could really talk to his dad, he cursed and muttered. 'And she's freakin' *hot*.'

Patch pursed his lips but his eyes danced with mischief. 'I might date younger women, but I'd never look at my second daughter and think she's hot. But I can see why my healthy son would think so. He might notice that she's grown up very well and has a killer bod.'

Seb twisted his lips. 'And I have a killer hard-on for her.'

Patch let out a low, rumbling laugh. 'Oh, geez, this is not going to end well. Especially since your modus is to bag her, tag her, and send her on her way when you're done with her. Isn't that the way you roll?'

Crude, but true.

'And if you hurt her I'll kick your ass,' Patch added.

Seb rolled his head around in an effort to relieve the knots he'd discovered in his shoulders and neck since Rowan had moved into his life. 'We have a history. My sister is her best friend. Her parents are important to me. I don't particularly like her; she's everything I'd run from in any other woman. Unconventional, free-spirited, slightly eccentric. And I forget all that every time I look at her. All I want to do is—'

'Don't say it.' Patch held up his hand and grimaced. 'Like Callie, I prefer to think of her as untouched and un-sullied.'

'Hypocrite.' Seb laughed and then turned contemplative. 'I've never had such a strong reaction to any woman—ever. So why her and why now?'

'It's fate bitch-slapping you. It likes to do that.'

'Sucker-punching, more like it.' Seb picked up his oar and dipped it into the sea. He glanced over to Patch as they easily covered the gap between them and the group. 'No pithy words of advice?'

'From me? The king of bad decisions pertaining to women? Nah! I'm just going to sit back and enjoy watching you making a fool of yourself over this girl.'

'That's not going to happen. My brain is still firmly in charge of my junk,' Seb lied through his teeth.

Patrick's deep laugh rippled across the sea. 'Yeah, you keep telling yourself that, my boy!'

'Thanks for your help,' Seb said dryly. 'I'm going to head back. Which bed are you sleeping in tonight?'

'The cottage, since crazy Miranda changed the locks on my house.' Patch shrugged. 'I'm really going to have to do something about her soon.'

'You think?' Seb did a quick turn, slapped Patch's hand and started to paddle away. His dad's soft words had him looking back.

'Is she okay? Your mum? I know that you…check up on her now and again.'

Seb blew out his breath. 'As far as I can tell, Dad.'

'Where?'

'South America.'

Patch suddenly looked every one of his sixty-plus years. 'Ro's not like Laura, Seb. She's kinder, smarter, less self-involved.' Patch dipped his paddle into the water and launched a stream of water into Seb's face. 'Go on—get out of here.'

CHAPTER FIVE

WHEN HE WALKED into his kitchen forty minutes later—sweat-slicked and puffing—and saw Rowan bending over the kitchen sink, eating a juicy peach, he knew that Patch was right about his brain not being in control.

In fact it pretty much dissolved as he watched her from outside the door. Juice dripped down her chin and down her toned, tanned arms. She'd pulled her hair up into a messy knot and wore a lumo-purple bikini, the bottom half of which was covered by a thin multi-coloured wrap. Thanks to the afternoon sun pouring into the kitchen he could see the outline of her legs beneath the wrap, the shape of her hips, the rounded perfection of her butt. Sunlight on her back illuminated her spine, the soft skin between her jaw and neck, the slope of her thin shoulders.

Unaware that he stood there, she groaned as she bit into the peach again and more juice dripped.

He didn't—couldn't—think. His feet moved of their own accord, his hand whipped out to grab her hips and spin her around, and his mouth slammed onto hers. Peach juice, warm and sweet, thundered over his tongue, quickly followed by the taste of Rowan, as sweet and a hundred times spicier. He thought he heard—felt?—her squeak of surprise, but he didn't care; all he needed was to taste her, to feel her breasts flattened against his chest, her pelvis lifting into his to ride his erection.

Seb hooked his hand around her thigh and yanked her leg upwards, mentally cursed when her thigh encountered the barrier of her wrap. Without leaving her mouth—how could he?—he dropped his hands and fumbled at the loose knot at her hips. He needed to feel her, taste her, consume her… This was madness and fiercely unstoppable.

Unable to undo the knot, he pushed his thumbs between the fabric and her hips and shimmied it down so that it fell into a rainbow at her feet. Plastering his hands on her back, on her butt, he yanked her even closer until he doubted they could slip a piece of paper between them.

And, miracle of miracles, she was as into the kiss as he was. Little nips here. A long slide of her tongue there. Small hands were exploring his bare chest, down his ribcage, over his obliques and around to his back. She linked her arms around his neck and he was dimly aware that she still held the half-eaten peach in her hand, the juice from which was dripping down his back.

She could lick it off… She could lick anywhere she wanted to. Hopefully the thought would occur to her…

It was like being caught up in a hot, sexy, whippy storm, Rowan thought. One moment she'd had a peach in her hands and mouth, the next moment they were filled with a hard, sweaty, sexy man.

With the peach still in her hand she made a sticky path of juice across his shoulder, down his pec and over a flat nipple, lightly covered in blond hair. Dropping her head, she watched a bead of juice hit that nubby surface and shot her tongue out and licked it up, sighing as she tasted the saltiness of his skin, felt his muscles contract under her tongue.

'What's good for the goose…' Seb muttered, pulling the half-eaten fruit from her hand.

Rowan's eyes clouded over as he pulled the triangle of fabric covering her right breast away and touched her with

the tips of his fingers, tanned against her much lighter skin.
Her eyes watched his intense concentration as he played
with her breast, running the wet peach over her distended
nipple, alternating with subtle brushes of his thumb.

'To hell with this.'

Seb tossed the peach onto the floor, wrapped one strong
arm around her bottom and, with the other arm, lifted her
onto the dining room table, yanking the chair out of his
way. Rowan barely noticed that the chair had toppled over
and clattered to the floor because Seb's warm tongue was
curled around her nipple and his other hand was burrow-
ing into the back of her bikini pants, tracing erotic pat-
terns on her butt.

He claimed her mouth again in a kiss that flew past
heated and went straight to molten. Her legs, operating
independently, hooked themselves around his waist and
she scooted closer to him to feel that hard ridge against
her mound.

Nothing else was important but to feel Seb, taste him,
know him.

Seb pulled his mouth away and his hands, still on her
breast and her butt, stilled. 'Point of no return, Ro. Yes or
no?'

Like she had a choice, Ro thought, dazed. There was
only one answer and her body was screaming it. 'Yes. Now.'

'Here?' Seb demanded.

She couldn't wait—had no patience to climb the stairs
to a bedroom, to spare the couple of minutes that would
take. 'Here. Now. Please.'

Seb muttered a curse and tried to step away. Rowan
slapped a hand against the back of his neck and dragged
him into a kiss that caused their feet to curl.

Seb yanked his mouth away and held up his hands. 'Ro,
one sec…condom.'

Rowan bounced on the dining room table, her body one

long electrical current. 'If you have to go upstairs for one I'm coming with you,' she told him, deadly serious.

'There's a deal.' Seb picked up his wallet from the counter near the door and cards and cash were scattered over the floor. 'There should be one in here. Bingo.'

He held it up in his fingers as he stood between her legs again. 'You going to do the honours or must I?'

Rowan smiled slow and deep as she pulled the little packet from his fingers. 'Oh, I think I will. Why don't you make yourself useful and get me naked?'

Seb nipped the corner of her mouth as she pushed his running shorts over his erection, down his hips. 'That's a hell of an offer, Brat.'

Rowan sighed as her fingers whispered the latex over him, encircling all that masculine strength in her fist. 'I'm a hell of a girl, Hollis. Now, why don't we slide your Part A into my Plot B and see if we fit?'

The luminous hands on the bedside clock informed Rowan that it was past midnight as she rolled over onto her stomach to watch Seb walk into his *en-suite* bathroom. She'd been in Seb's arms, in his bed, for more than six hours. Six hours of intense, bone-dissolving, earth-spinning pleasure. She was one gooey, sexy mess and she wanted nothing more than to roll over and drift off to sleep.

Instead, she forced herself to sit up, then stand… Ooh, wobbly legs. The nearest garment was one of Seb's T-shirts and she pulled it over her head, unable to stop herself from sniffing the collar for that special combination of soap and cologne that she couldn't get enough of.

Just as she couldn't get enough of his kisses, of the feel of his hard muscles under her hands, the way she felt… *complete* when he slid inside her.

In between their lovemaking they'd dozed, before one

of them reached out for another kiss, another stroke, and they fell into passion again...

It was time to face reality. She didn't want to, but she had to.

She didn't know how to do this. She didn't do this... Well, she had—but not enough to feel comfortable waking up naked in his bed, with his room looking as if a hurricane had hit it after them rolling around like maniacs and bouncing off the furniture. She didn't want to stay but she couldn't just leave.

She really, really needed to polish up on her one-night stand etiquette.

And a one-night stand was all it was—all it could ever be. She had to be sensible about this... This was sex. Nothing more. They had acted on impulse, had used each other's bodies for brief, intense pleasure. It wasn't anything more—could never be anything more...

Rowan placed the balls of her hands into her eyes and pushed. It was okay, she told herself. She was allowed to have sex with a single man. The world hadn't stopped spinning. Wasn't free choice high on her list of values? She hadn't agreed to anything more than one night, to a casual hook-up, a night of pleasure.

It didn't change anything... In a couple of weeks her parents would be back. She'd say hello and how are you doing, make nice, and then she'd borrow that money from Seb and fly away. Because that was what she did best: she flew, caught trains, ox-carts, buses... That was how she lived her life. She didn't stay in one place, in one house, couldn't imagine a steady life with one man.

Staying still, coming face to face and heart to heart with a man terrified her. Mostly because she'd been disappointing people all her life and she'd have to love a man very much to stay still. The thought of losing her freedom—so hard earned—caused a cold, hard ball of something *icky* to form in her stomach.

She should leave, go back to her own room…take some time to regain her equilibrium.

'God, you look like someone shot your favourite dog,' Seb said from the doorway of the *en-suite* bathroom.

Rowan's eyes shot up and met his. Earlier they'd been warm with desire, laughter. Now they were cool and flat, and his expression was guarded and remote. Ah, so she wasn't the only one in the room having second—or third— thoughts.

Good to know.

'Ah… I was just…' Rowan placed her hands on her hips and looked around.

'Leaving?'

Since she was clear across the room and two feet from the door, what was the point in lying? 'Yeah…'

Was it her imagination or did she see his face harden? It was hard to tell in the dim light spilling from the bathroom.

'No cuddling required? After-dinner pillow-talk?'

Oh, that was sarcastic, and it blew any of her few remaining warm and fuzzies away. The problem was that there was a part of her that would have loved a cuddle, a gentle hand down her back, listening to his heartbeat under her ear, drifting off to the sound of him breathing next to her…

Because she felt weak and vulnerable—girly—she gave herself a mental slap and straightened her spine.

'Do you need pillow-talk and cuddling?' Rowan demanded, equally facetious.

'Of course I don't,' Seb ground out, walking naked back into the room.

There was no point in feeling embarrassed, Rowan realised, since she'd explored most, if not all of that luscious body. He had a swimmer's build, broad shoulders, slim hips, muscular thighs.

Rowan felt she should say something to dissipate the heavy, soggy blanket of emotional tension in the room. 'Look, Seb, you don't need to get all weirded out by this… I'm not going to get all hearts and flowers over you.'

'Oh, goody.'

Sarcastic again. He did it so well. 'For someone who is anti-commitment, and who doesn't do emotional connections, I would've thought that me leaving and getting out of your face would be the perfect scenario for you.'

'Yep, you'd think,' Seb said, in that bland voice that made her itch to smack him.

Rowan threw up her hands. 'How can we be so great in bed but so pathetically useless at actual talking?'

'Beats me.'

'You're ticked because your big brain is running at warp speed, trying to rationalise this, trying to intellectualise what just happened. You're frustrated because you don't understand how you can have mind-blowing sex with a woman you're not sure you like and who has driven you nuts your entire life.'

'I am not doing anything of the sort!' Seb retorted.

But Rowan caught the flicker of guilt in his eyes. Of course he was. She sighed. It was what Seb did. When something caught him off guard he put his extraordinary intellect to work and tried to figure it out on a cerebral level. Hadn't she watched him do exactly that growing up? She and Callie would wail and whine when things went wrong. Seb and her brother Peter would ignore the emotion and look for the cause and effect.

Men are from Mars, indeed…

'Your brain is going to explode. Attraction and lust can't be measured, analysed, categorised. It just *is*—like some things just are,' Rowan said softly. 'It was just sex, Seb, not quantum physics.'

'Yeah, whatever.'

Seb made a production out of yawning, pulled back the covers on his bed and flicked her a quick glance before climbing into bed.

'I'm going to sleep. Night.'

Rowan narrowed her eyes at him as he punched the pillows before rolling over and snuggling down. No *Thanks for a fun time*? No *See you in the morning*? He couldn't be more clinical about it if he left a couple of notes on the dresser table...

No—*no!*—that wasn't fair.

Be honest, here, Dunn. You were the one who set the tone for the way this ended... You were heading out of the door when he returned to the room. You were running scared and saying that you didn't need the mushy stuff...

And you don't.

You don't need anything but to research your netsuke, gather some cash, say a brief hello to your folks and high-tail it back to...where? London? Canada? South America?

You need to be free, on the road, responsible to no one but yourself.

Rowan sent Seb one more look—was that snoring she heard? Really?—and half banged, half slammed his bedroom door closed.

Tangling with him had been fun physically, but mentally—huh! A toxic spill...

His brain, when blood finally reached it, was red-lining, Seb decided as the door banged shut behind Rowan and his eyes flew open. He was doing exactly what she'd said: intellectualising, categorising, analysing. He didn't understand what had happened earlier—that tsunami of want and need and pure animal instinct. He was a rational and stable guy. He didn't get caught up in the moment or swept away by passion.

He needed to understand why it had happened tonight

with Ro. He had to understand. Because if he could com-
prehend it then he would regain control of the situation.
It was his modus operandi—the way he approached and
dealt with life, with his problems. When his mum had left
he'd expected her home within a month, then three, then
six. The only way for him to deal with the slow-dawning
reality that he and Callie had been essentially abandoned
by the person who was supposed to love them most had
been to rationalise it, to find a plausible—though mostly
improbable—explanation.

*She was ill and couldn't come home. She'd been kid-
napped by Colombian drug lords and/or an alien space
ship. She was an international spy.*

He'd think it through, dissect the problem, and in that
way he could subdue the bubbling, unpredictable mess emotions generated.

He didn't cope well with unpredictable and messy emotions.

And Rowan was five-foot-four of unpredictable and
messy.

And why on earth did he feel ticked because Rowan
didn't want to spend the rest of the night in his bed? Didn't
want to be held? Her reaction should have him slipping off
to sleep guilt-free, with a satisfied body and a huge smile
on his face. Instead he was lying here like a freaking moron
wanting...*what?* He cursed. Was he actually considering
wading into messy and unpredictable?

Was that what had sent his brain into hyper-drive?

It couldn't possibly be, he decided. *You don't do emotional and you don't do connections, Butt-face.* And, really,
if he decided that was something he suddenly wanted—
through alien possession or a punch to his head—why
would he choose a world-wanderer who couldn't stay in
one place for more than a heartbeat? Choose a connection
with someone who, when the thrill of those first couple of

weeks wore off and the excitement of great sex started to fade away, would be on the first plane…

Oh, wait…he was going to lend her the money to do that anyway!

Seb stood up and walked back into the bathroom, gripped the edge of the counter. It shouldn't be this way, he thought. He should be glad that she'd walked out through that door and left him alone—instead of feeling as if he wanted to go to her, pull her back to his bed, fall asleep and wake her up by making love to her again. Again…why was he wondering whether they could connect on some sort of intellectual level as well as they did in the sack?

It didn't matter… Bottom line, he shouldn't be thinking about her this way. She'd been a good way to spend the night—an exceptional way to spend the night.

His junk twitched and pulsed at the memory of her… under him, over him…her hair brushing his chest, her warmth enclosing him like a warm, wet perfect glove…

Oh, hell, now he was never going to get to sleep with those thoughts rattling around in his head.

Seb walked back into his room and saw the shadows of his computers sitting in the far corner of his room.

Okay, well…he might as well give his big brain some work to do.

The following evening Seb stood just outside his front door and watched as Rowan, standing in front of the antique mirror in the hallway, tugged at the short white T-shirt that showed an inch of her waist above black low-slung jeans. Good grief, she looked hot!

They hadn't seen each other since their awkward goodbye last night and, thanks to having to jump on the super-early flight to Durban this morning, he hadn't had a moment to touch base with her.

He'd thought that the meeting in Durban would be a

morning affair, but he'd run into some serious challenges—
his clients had been more paranoid than normal and had
required a lot of reassurance that their precious information was safe in his hands—and the entire day had been a
nightmare, with suits peering over his shoulder, checking
and rechecking his progress.

Blerch.

And Rowan hadn't reached out to make contact. Then
again, neither had he... Should he have? He didn't have
the faintest clue—mostly because women always chased
him. It was what they did. They normally followed up with
a BBM, an SMS, a hello-how-are-you-doing e-mail. But
Rowan? Nothing.

He was equally intrigued and annoyed...and didn't *that*
make him sound like an egotistical jerk? He'd thought about
calling to check up on her but he hadn't been sure what
to say.

He hadn't slept much and he rubbed his eyes with his
thumbs. Why was he still so wigged out about the way the
evening had panned out? Maybe it was because Rowan
had blown every perception he'd had about women and
sex out of the window.

He'd thought that most women needed some kind of
emotional connection to have sex—that they needed to talk
before and after. Rowan hadn't required before-sex cajoling
or after-sex reassurance and she'd approached the whole
experience like a guy would. Like he did.

It was a blessing in disguise that she hadn't needed him
to talk, because thanks to that damned peach and the see-
through wrap his tongue wouldn't have been able to form
the words.

She was keeping him at an emotional distance, they'd
had sex and practically no conversation—which he normally considered the ideal relationship—and it bugged the
crap out of him.

Could he say hypocritical and bastard and then put them together in a sentence?

Rowan jumped as he stepped into the hall. Dropping his laptop and briefcase onto the old yellow wood table, he pulled off his wire-rimmed glasses, tossed them down and raised his eyebrows at Rowan. 'Going somewhere?'

To keep from tugging her shirt down, Rowan shoved her hands into the pockets of her jeans and rocked on her heels. 'Hi. You're…back.'

'It is Friday night,' Seb pointed out. And it was his house.

'I thought you might have plans—like a date,' Rowan said to his back as he disappeared down the passage.

He was back in under a minute, a bottle of beer in his hand. A date? He'd slept with her last night and she had him already trawling for another woman?

He didn't know whether to be ticked or flattered that she thought him to be such a player. Seb thought for a moment; nah, he was definitely POed.

'My plans? Nothing more strenuous than a burger, a beer and an early night. It's the Fish and Fern tomorrow.'

Rowan wrinkled her nose. 'The what?'

Seb gave her a long look before emptying his pockets, placing his mobile, keys and a thin wallet on the table. 'The triathlon race. The one on the fridge. Swimming, running, biking?'

'Oh, right. What time do you think you'll be home?'

Seb shrugged. 'Eight-ish, I suppose. There's a barbecue after the prize-giving and I'll probably stay for that. Problem?'

'No.'

Rowan tugged the shirt down but it sprang up her tummy with all the obstinacy of stretched cotton. He clocked her tousled but elaborate hairdo, the subtle make-up, the bangles at her wrist and the beaded earrings. She looked as if *she* was going on a date… Was that why she'd asked him whether he had plans? Because she did?

Hell, no. That wasn't happening.

'So, what are *you* up to tonight? That's one heck of an outfit, by the way.'

Rowan responded to the thinly disguised annoyance in his tone by raising her chin. 'What's wrong with my outfit?'

'Tight low-rise jeans, short top, fixed hair. Wherever you're going, you are going to get hit on all night.' The beer was not doing the trick of relaxing him; Rowan changing and staying at home would.

'Don't be ridiculous.'

'I'm a guy and I know exactly what *I'd* read into your outfit.'

'Guys would read sex into a nun's habit.'

He noticed that she still hadn't told him where she was going. What was the big deal? His temper, on a low simmer all day, started to heat. He shrugged out of his jacket and threw it over the newel post of the staircase. He yanked his pale green dress shirt out of his black pants and sat on the bottom stair to pull off his shoes.

Seb rested his elbows on the stair above, took a long sip of his beer and picked up a shovel to dig his own grave. 'So, where are you going? And who are you going with?'

'I'm going to a bar.'

'A bar?'

'You make it sound as if I am about to do a deal with the local meth supplier! I feel like I've been catapulted back to my teenage years with my over-protective parents. I'm not sixteen any more, Seb. What is your problem?' Rowan demanded when he just looked past her in stony silence. 'Why are you acting like this?'

Fair question.

'I didn't expect to come home to…' Seb rubbed his temple '…this.'

'This?' Rowan felt the bubbles of her temper rise to the surface and pop. '"This" being jeans and a tee?'

'"This" being you dressed up and looking hot.'

'I did my hair and put on some make-up…this is pretty normal!'

'Nothing about you is normal!' Seb sprang up, his eyes tired and sparking. 'Do you know how sexy you look? You'll have every male tongue dropping to the floor in that bar. You were mine last night and the thought of you going out and being someone else's is making me want to punch something.'

As soon as the words left his mouth and their meaning sank in Seb knew that he'd made a crucial mistake—that he'd been a total tool. Her eyes shimmered with hurt and she bit her lip to keep it from wobbling. He *never* spoke without thinking, but those words had just bubbled up, over and out…

Seb swore at himself and ran an agitated hand through his hair.

'Excuse me?'

Oh, crap. She'd kicked 'hurt' into the back seat and now she was seriously ticked. Wonderful. And could he blame her?

Seb twisted his lips and thought he'd attempt to explain. 'Okay, look, that came out wrong…'

'You think I am so easy that I could jump from your bed to someone else's?' Rowan laughed and the sound didn't hold a teaspoonful of mirth. She held up a hand. 'No, don't answer that, because I'm very close to smacking you silly! What a joke!'

If it was, he failed to see it.

Rowan shook her head, snapped a set of car keys off the hall table and picked up the bag that she'd hung on the coat stand. She walked towards the door.

Seb was thinking of how to keep her in the room when

she turned around abruptly and looked at him with blazing eyes. 'No, I'm not going to do this again.'

'Do what?'

'Leave you to your assumptions. I think that's a mistake I keep making over and over with you and my family. I allow you to jump to these crazy assumptions about me because…because of habit, maybe. Pride, maybe. But this—you thinking that I treat sex casually just because we had a great time in the sack—I can't let this ride. The reason we had great sex is because we obviously—who knows why?—have amazing chemistry. Why we have this chemistry when I think you have the personality and charm of a horse's ass is a mystery for another day.'

'I—'

'My turn.' Rowan cut him off with a sharp wave of her hand. 'As for my sexual history—do you know how hard it is, as a female travelling on her own, to get laid?'

She looked as if she was waiting for a response so Seb thought it was safe to say: 'Uh…no?'

Rowan looked momentarily triumphant. 'Hah! Of course you don't. You just assume that it's what we travellers do.' Her chest rose and fell with temper. 'Every man I meet—all the time—is a stranger. I don't know him. I'm not given the time to know him. I can think he's cute, but psychos come cute as well. Now, say I decide to take a chance… I have to get into a room with him—because, you know, I like a bit of privacy with my sex. That means I put myself in danger every time. And do you want to know how many times I've done that?'

Seb, now feeling like a first-prize fool, shrugged.

'None, Seb. I've *never* done it. I've had a couple of relationships over the years with guys I've known for a long time. I don't do hook-ups. It's a dangerous and stupid thing to do when you don't have any friends or family to rescue you if something goes horribly wrong.'

Seb scrubbed his face with his hands, feeling equally relieved and foolish.

'And, just so that I'm very clear about this, *we* rocked it because you have a heck of a bod and you are a good kisser and I haven't had any for a while.'

Okay, how deep was that hole he'd dug for himself and when could he throw himself into it?

But Rowan wasn't quite finished; she still had another layer of skin to strip off him. 'And I'm not going *to* a bar, you moron. I've got a job *tending* bar so that I can make some cash to pay you back and get out of your stupid, judgmental face!'

With that last verbal slap—which he so deserved— Rowan turned on her heel and walked out of his house.

CHAPTER SIX

ROWAN, EXHAUSTED AND smelling of beer and bar, walked back into the hall of Awelfor shortly after twelve-thirty and sighed when she saw Seb standing in the doorway to the small TV lounge, dressed in casual track pants and a loose-fitting T-shirt.

She was still feeling raw, hurt and angry that Seb—smart, smart Seb, who apparently had the emotional intelligence of an amoeba—had assumed that she was back-packing baggage with the morals of an alley cat. She was exhausted from not sleeping much last night, from career-ing around Cape Town today picking up all the equipment she needed—haybales, paint guns, food—for the party the next day, and she was depressed that she hadn't had a sec-ond to research the netsuke and that she'd been reduced to serving beers and martinis again. Dammit, she was twenty-eight years old—not nineteen.

'I don't want to fight, Seb.' Rowan dropped her bag to the floor and rubbed the back of her neck. 'If you're going to take any more shots at me, can I ask that you do it in the morning? I'm wiped out.'

'Come in here for a moment.'

Rowan cursed silently as he walked away without waiting for her response. *Let's just get this over with,* she thought, following him into the messy room. A large screen, big boys' TV dominated one wall and dark choco-

late leather couches, long and wide enough to accommodate his large frame, were placed in an L-shape in front of
the screen. A wooden coffee table held a large laptop and
a bottle of red wine and two glasses.

Seb lifted the bottle and filled a glass, topping up his
own half-full glass after he did so. He handed her the glass
and nodded to the couch. Rowan, figuring that it was easier just to take the glass and sit down rather than argue
with him, dropped to the couch and sighed as the pressure
eased off her feet. She had forgotten how hard bartending
was on the feet.

Seb sat down on the coffee table in front of her, his knees
brushing hers. He held his wine glass between his knees
and stared at the brown and cream carpet beneath him.

'I owe you the biggest apology.'

Okay, she knew she was tired, but was she really hearing Seb correctly? He was apologising? Seriously?

'Saying what I did earlier was…unkind and ugly and…
Sorry. I really didn't mean it. It was a stupid off-the-cuff-
comment that slipped out because I was annoyed and tired
and not thinking.'

'Now, there's a first—you not thinking,' Rowan teased,
and Seb's face was transformed by a relieved smile.

Seb dropped a casual hand onto her knee. 'Friends?'

'Can we possibly be?' Rowan asked him, cocking her
head and looking into those dark blue eyes.

Seb tugged on his bottom lip, placed his glass on the
table next to his powerful thigh and put his elbows on his
knees. 'Your verbal slap about making assumptions also hit
home. Although I never believed those drugs were yours,
I *did* think that you were reckless and rebellious and irresponsible as a kid.'

'I *was* reckless and rebellious and irresponsible as a kid,'
Rowan pointed out.

'But I carried on assuming that. I didn't think that you

had changed, that you'd grown up. There's so much that I—we—all of us—don't know about you. I don't know you and I wonder if I ever did.'

Rowan felt her throat tighten. Finally. Finally someone from her past was looking at her differently, trying to see her and not the person they wanted her to be. Rowan put her fist to her lips and nibbled at the skin on her index finger. And, in fairness, how much did she know about *him*? About any of them? Surface stuff. Social media stuff. And how much of that was the truth?

She had to have some preconceived ideas about him and her family that weren't based in reality either.

'So, how about we try to get to know the grown-up versions of ourselves?' Seb suggested.

There was nothing she wanted more. Acceptance and understanding. While she craved her freedom, she also wanted the freedom to be herself in this place where she'd always felt she could never be that.

Rowan dropped her hand and picked up her glass with a shaky hand. 'I'd like that, but…'

'But?'

'But what about the other thing? The last night thing?'

'Sex?' Seb lifted his glass, drained half its contents and tapped his finger against the crystal. 'Let's not make this any more complicated than it has to be. What if we just put that onto the back burner for now and try to be friends?'

Rowan's smile was wide and true. 'Okay, let's try that.'

'Good.' Seb placed his hands on the table behind him and leaned back. 'And, as your friend, I'm going to ask you something.'

Rowan groaned theatrically. 'Oh, no.'

'Why haven't you been home? Why haven't you popped your head through the fence, looked at your house, walked through the gardens? Said hello to the dogs?'

'New dogs. They don't know me.'

'Hedging, Ro.'

'The house is occupied, Seb. I can't just go wandering through.'

'Hedging. I told the occupiers that you were home and not to worry if they saw you hovering around. They were cool about it. So, again, hedging…'

She was, and she didn't know what to say. She'd been avoiding going home because that way she could avoid thinking about her parents, about what she'd say to them when she saw them again, what they would say to her. And the truth was seeing the house made her remember how unhappy—no, not unhappy, just how excluded she'd felt from her family. Her parents and brother had been so close, sharing the same interests, the same quest for knowledge and mental improvement.

It made her feel eighteen again and all at sea.

'Were you so miserable at home, Ro?'

'Miserable? No.' Rowan looked around. 'But I always felt so much more at home here in Awelfor. Here I could dance and sing and laugh loudly…home was so quiet.'

Seb smiled. 'And you were the most lively child we knew.'

'I suppose I should take a look at the house… I can't avoid it for ever.' Rowan brushed her hair back. 'I don't know what I'm going to say to my parents, Seb. Should I apologise for living my own life? For not coming back for so long?'

'Did you want to?'

Rowan shook her head. 'No, I wasn't ready to come home. Didn't feel strong enough.'

'Then don't apologise, Ro.' Seb leaned forward and rested his elbows on his knees. 'I've been listening to your folks—mostly your dad—moaning about your travelling for years, but tonight for the first time I looked at it from another angle. Your parents are wealthy enough to travel and you've always returned to London. They could've met you there, or anywhere else, quite a few times during the last decade.'

'I've thought about that often,' Rowan admitted in a whisper. 'Why didn't they do that?'

'Because they didn't want you there; they wanted you here. Because it would have given you their tacit approval of your travelling, for choosing your own way of life, if they did that.' Seb grimaced. 'I like your parents, Ro. They were good to me growing up. But I could engage them on an intellectual level. As Patch said, you were always way too emotional for them.'

'Patch said that? I love that man.'

'I do too. He's been the best dad—apart from his habit of dating too-young, too-stupid-to-live gold-diggers.'

Rowan laughed, loosely linked one arm around Seb's neck and placed her cheek to his. 'I like this—talking to you. I think it's the first proper conversation we've had.'

'And I'm pretty sure that it's snowing in hell.' Seb ran his hand down Rowan's back before pulling away. 'You need to go home, Ro. Take a look. Confront those demons. They aren't as big as you think. And you need to go to bed—because if you don't I'm going to become very unfriendly and kiss you stupid.'

Rowan pulled her head back and her eyes were smoky with passion. 'I was thinking exactly the same thing.' She stood up and scooted around his legs. 'Sleep well, Seb.'

'You too, Brat.'

Rowan handed out the last goodie bag, ruffled the last head and placed her hands on her hips as she watched the last expensive car—this one was a Bentley—cruise away.

Thank God, thank God, thank God! Rowan felt almost dizzy with relief. Hauling the envelope out of her back pocket, she took out the cash and nearly did a happy dance in the middle of the driveway. Annie's son and daughter-in-law, although taken aback by their very muddy, very happy boy, had instantly recognised by his jabbering, excited conversation that his party had been a huge success. His father, his neck pulled forward by the rope-thick gold chain around his neck, had added a bonus of five hundred to the highway robbery price Annie had already paid her.

Three other mummies, obviously in awe of Seb's property, had asked for her business card. Not having one, she'd hastily scribbled her contact details on a serviette.

Professional, she was not.

But the cake had been perfect, and the mini-quadbikes and paintball shooting had been fun. She'd had her own gun and was supposed to be treated like Switzerland—but all that meant was that the rug-rats had had a common enemy and had shot at her whenever the opportunity arose. She had a bright purple paint mark on her neck and her T-shirt, jeans and legs were multi-coloured blotches.

Looking towards the paddock, she noticed that the hay-bales and used car tyres that had formed the track for the mini-quadbikes, as well as Seb's white fence poles, were splattered as well. Nothing that a hosepipe or a good thunderstorm couldn't fix... Rowan looked up at the sky and cursed the lack of clouds. She was exhausted already, and she had the kitchen to clean up. She didn't feel like hosing down the poles as well.

Crab-fishing in the stream at the bottom of the property had been another highlight of the day. It had been a bit of a problem finding enough branches to make adequate poles, and she had sacrificed a nice piece of fillet steak she'd found in the fridge to use as bait, but they had pulled up a lot of the unwelcome creatures that populated the small stream.

None of the kids had got hurt, lost or even cried. They'd had enough sugar to put them on a high for days, had a whole lot of fun, and if their parents had to throw away their mud-and paint-stained designer clothes Rowan was pretty sure they could afford to buy more. She had some cash in her pocket and she felt a sense of accomplishment that was different from buying and selling.

It was being around innocence, having fun doing the simple things she'd done with Callie, feeding off the kids' joyous energy. She'd run, skipped, hopped, climbed and crawled, and she'd frequently thought that she couldn't believe she was getting paid to have this much fun.

Kids. Not having had much to do with them, she would never have believed that she would enjoy them so much.

Rowan grimaced as she sank onto the bottom of the four steps that led to the wide veranda. She rubbed her lower back—she'd tumbled backwards off a stack of hay-bales and was now paying the price—and rested her aching head against the stone wall. She'd had minimal sleep over the past few days—sleeping with Seb and bartending had both translated into very late nights—and she'd been up with the sparrows this morning to get everything done before the kids arrived.

She shouldn't have stopped, shouldn't have sat down Now that she knew how tired she was she didn't think she could find the energy to get up, never mind clear up the mess that the kids had made and the disaster area that was the kitchen. She'd just sit here for a minute with her eyes closed and try to recharge her batteries...

When Seb shook her awake the sun was dipping behind the mountains and she felt slightly chilly. She yawned as she glanced up at him, still dressed in his exercise gear, although he'd pulled on a hooded sweatshirt. Seb held out his hand and pulled her to her feet.

'I've made tea,' he said, leading her by the hand to the kitchen.

'You hate tea,' Rowan said on a smothered yawn.

'Not for me, for you.' Seb pulled out a chair from the table and shoved her into it.

As her eyes focused Rowan noticed that, instead of looking as if a nuclear bomb had exploded in it, the kitchen was tidy, all the surfaces were clean, the chip and sweet packets were packed away and the remains of the cake were in a big plastic container.

'You cleaned up.' Rowan took the cup he held out and wrapped her hands around it. 'You shouldn't have. I was going to.'

'Anyone who could fall asleep against a stone pillar for an hour was not up to cleaning up.' Seb held a cup of coffee in one hand, his fingers curled around the mug.

Rowan wished, passionately, that they were curled around something attached to her.

'So, that was your function?'

'Mmm. My stupid way to make some money.'

'If it's legal, there is no stupid way to make money,' Seb responded. 'Was it worth it?'

Rowan nodded. 'Yes, it was. Do you mind your property being invaded by a horde of kids? They didn't come into the house, by the way, except to use the downstairs bathroom.'

'No, of course I don't mind,' Seb said, and shook his head at her puzzled look. When he spoke again, he sounded frustrated. 'Ro, you could fill this place with a hundred kids and I wouldn't mind. I *do* mind you working so hard that you fall asleep with your head on the wall as soon as you sit down. You coming home is supposed to give you some space to sort your life out, but you're bartending and arranging kids' parties and you're exhausted. You don't need to do this...'

'I need to earn some money, Seb. Quickly. I hate being...'

Seb waited through her silence, then added his own words. 'Beholden? In my debt? That's such crap, Ro. You're sleeping in a bed that isn't being used, you don't eat enough to feed a mouse, and you are housekeeping...'

Rowan looked around at the neat kitchen. 'I pack the dishwasher and I throw a load of laundry into the machine...it's hardly housekeeping.'

'True; any chance of you actually mopping anything?'

'Maybe.' Rowan blew a tendril of hair away from her mouth and stared down into her strong tea. 'Worse than feeling in your debt is feeling that I'm trapped. That I'm in this city, this place, this house, and I can't leave. It makes me feel...panicky.'

Seb pulled out a chair and sat down opposite her, wincing as he did so. 'Why? Why is being here so difficult for you?'

'Because I am so free out there, and when I am free I'm happy. Being here just makes me remember how controlling and protective my folks were, and...'

'They were trying to protect you, Rowan. From yourself, mostly.'

Rowan sighed. 'You always defend them...' She held up her hand to hold off his hot reply. 'I don't want to argue with you, Seb. I know that you think that they were good parents because yours—'

'Mine weren't. Well, Patch was okay. My mother was a train wreck.'

'Patch gave you freedom to move, to explore. I was never allowed beyond the walls of our two houses.'

'They—'

Rowan interrupted him. 'My point is that whether the ties that bind are silk scarves or barbed wire you still can't move, and I've always had the need to be unconstrained, unfettered...free.' Rowan sipped her tea. 'That makes me jittery, but coming home broke just makes me mad. I wanted to show them that I am successful, together...responsible. Not in their way but in *my* way. Now they are going to hear that I'm broke and homeless, they'll roll their eyes and launch into one of their what-did-we-do-wrong? speeches.' Sadness swept across her face. 'Do you think I could've been adopted and they never told me?'

'Considering the fact that you look exactly like your mum, I'd say the chances are slim,' Seb said, his tone bone-dry.

'It's just that I couldn't be more different to them if I tried.'

Seb stroked a hand over her head. 'Different isn't bad, Ro, it's just different. I'd like to believe that they'd like to be part of your life but have no idea how to achieve that— especially since you hop around the world like a schizoid bunny.'

Rowan glared at him.

'Have you ever thought about how scary your life must be to them? To them, going to London was a massive challenge: the crowds, the congestion, the unfamiliarity of a new city. You do that all the time. They would be terrified to live your type of life. They are not as brave as you, Ro.'

She'd never thought about her parents from that angle and she realised that Seb was right. Her parents thought that going to their timeshare unit up the coast was a mammoth undertaking, so going to London would be equivalent to going to the moon. Doing what she did would be, to them, inconceivable.

She understood that. But why couldn't *they* understand that while they needed to stay in their cocoon she needed to be free.

'Why did they go? I haven't even asked.'

'Your dad was asked to present a paper at some conference and Peter was going to meet them in the UK.' Seb wriggled in his chair, winced again, and Rowan frowned.

'What have you done to yourself?' she demanded.

'Tumbled down a hill on the trail run.' Seb took a sip

of his coffee and stood up. Taking a bread knife from the drawer, he lifted the lid off the container holding the cake and cut two healthy slices. Putting them onto the lid of the container, he carried it back to the table and slid the lid between them. Sitting again, he snapped off a square and shoved it into his mouth. 'Yasmeen's chocolate cake. God, that tastes good. Who made it?'

'How do you know I didn't make it, using her recipe?' Rowan asked indignantly.

'Because I've tasted enough of your disastrous cakes to last me a lifetime. I don't think you ever made one that tasted like…well, like cake.'

'You're right. I didn't make it. I found a lovely lady who makes cakes, gave her a copy of Yas's recipe—'

'If she finds out, you'll hang,' Seb told her.

'Are you going to rat me out?' Rowan asked indignantly.

Seb smiled. 'She'll find out. She always does. None of us have ever been able to sneak anything past her.'

'I'll be out of the country by then,' Rowan replied, relieved.

'You poor, naïve, deluded child. You think that matters? If I could harness her powers I could rule the world.'

'I'll change my name and she won't find me. Anyway, if I do more parties I'll use this woman again.'

'More parties? You want to do it again?'

'Strangely, I enjoyed it.' Rowan lowered her cup. 'And it's really good money, Seb. Two of today's mummies said that they'd call me because they have parties they need to arrange. If they want them done in the next two weeks or so I'll do it.' Rowan forced herself to meet his eyes. 'Will you let me have them here?'

Seb stared down at the cake in his hand for the longest time. 'I'd like to say no, but I know that won't stop you. You'll just find another venue. So I'll say yes—with certain conditions attached.'

Rowan bit the inside of her lip and waited for his words.

'Do the parties, Ro, but with help. There is no way that you can keep an eye on thirty kids by yourself. And that blonde who was hanging around was as much help as a corkscrew in a bottle-free desert. I mean proper help. Someone who can lift chairs and move tables and carry stuff, run after the kids if necessary,' Seb said, his tone serious. 'No help, no party. Deal?'

'But where would I find someone to help?' Rowan demanded.

'There are lots of kids in the area looking for casual work,' Seb replied, breaking off another piece of cake. 'Or me.'

Rowan hooted with laughter. '*You'd* help?'

'If you needed me. It wouldn't be my first choice on how to spend my time, but if you needed my help I'd give it.'

And he would—of course he would. 'Okay, thanks. *If* I get another party and *if* I need help I'll ask for it.'

'Good.' Seb's face softened as he handed her a piece of cake. 'Eat.'

Rowan placed it on her saucer and shook her head. 'Yank down your track pants.'

'I thought we discussed this? We were going to be friends…'

'Stop being a jerk and let me see your injury,' Rowan stated patiently. 'Anyway, I've seen all you have, so it's a bit late for modesty.'

'Why?'

'Because you're in pain and I want to see what is causing it.'

'And congratulate it?' Seb grumbled.

'Of course. I live to see you hurting!' Rowan replied, her voice chock-full of sarcasm. 'Seb, you know how stubborn I can be, and I'm going to nag you until I get to see it.'

She *was* stubborn and she *would* nag.

Seb tipped his head back in frustration, thinking about the foot-and-a-half-long graze that ran from his buttock to his knee. His elbow also displayed the results of connecting with the ground at speed. After fifteen years of doing trail runs and triathlons he should know better than to hurtle down a mountainous track with his mind somewhere else—like in bed with Rowan.

It also burned that he'd been lying fourth at the time, feeling strong, with a good chance of catching the front runners. If he had seen that loose gravel right in front of his nose he would have finished the race—except that he'd broken the front joint on his bike as he'd tipped head over heels and had to retire. He hated not finishing a race almost as much as he hated not doing well.

He made the mistake of looking at Rowan, who was watching him...and waiting. For the love of God...

He pushed his track pants over his hips, stepped out of them and pulled up the back of his running shorts. He knew it looked bad when Rowan said nothing for a long time.

'It needs to be cleaned, and you can't reach to do it properly. Where's the first aid kit?'

Seb shook his head. 'If you think I'm going to let you come within a mile of me with a bottle of peroxide, you're mad.'

'First aid kit?'

'Ro, you're a better baker than you are a nurse!'

Rowan just folded her arms and tapped her foot and waited. Then she waited some more. Stubborn, obstinate and wilful; she gave a deeper meaning to those three words.

Giving in, with very bad grace, he stomped to the cupboard and lifted the first aid box from the top shelf. Banging it onto the kitchen table, he scowled at Rowan. 'Try not to kill me, Nurse Ratched.'

Rowan pulled her tongue at him before ordering him to

lie with his chest on the table and his legs stretched out. Doing as he was told, he felt like an idiot.

When nothing happened, Seb turned around to see her inspecting his leg. 'What's the problem?'

'Small pieces of stone and gravel are imbedded in the skin,' Rowan replied as she reached for the tweezers, the cotton wool and the peroxide bottle.

Seb gritted his teeth as she picked out pieces of stone and gravel. Taking a peroxide-wet cotton ball, she dabbed it over the spot and Seb swore viciously.

Rowan used the tweezers and dabbed again. Seb repeated the words.

He kept up his litany of swear words as Rowan tweezed the bigger pieces out.

A little while later he heard Rowan's stomach rumbling. 'So, any ideas about supper? I'm starving,' she said.

'Steak, potatoes and a green salad? Bloody hell, Ro!' Seb shouted, clenching every muscle in his body in pain as she worked on the area directly behind his knee.

Rowan stopped, glanced towards the fridge and pulled a face. 'Is that fillet steak?'

'Yes. Can you get a move on, please?' Seb demanded through a red haze of pain.

Rowan peered at the graze, and when she dropped the tweezers Seb realised that she was finally satisfied that he was stone-and dirt-free.

'Problem. I used your fillet steak to bait the hooks for crab-fishing.'

Seb turned his head and glared at her.

'Sorry,' Rowan responded, dousing another cotton ball in peroxide and swabbing it across his elbow this time.

Seb flew up, ripped the ball from her hand and launched it in the direction of the dustbin. 'You're having a bit too much fun at my expense, Rowan.'

Rowan met his hot eyes and clearly saw the mixture

of desire, frustration and amusement bubbling there. She licked her lips and risked lifting her hand to touch his cheek. 'Not fun, exactly. Maybe a tiny little bit of revenge for all those times you were so mean to me growing up.'

'You deserved everything I ever gave you,' Seb muttered, his gaze on her luscious mouth, wishing he could bend his head and cover it with his. He still wanted her... didn't think he'd ever stop wanting her.

Rowan, surprisingly, made the first move. Standing on her tiptoes, she brushed her lips against his, her tongue darting out to lick his bottom lip. His mouth softened as his hands gripped her upper arms. He started to pull her forward, to deepen the kiss...

Dammit! He couldn't do this—couldn't start something neither of them could finish. Seb placed his hands on her waist, lifted her up and away—as far away from him as possible—and dumped her, bottom first, on the kitchen table. He reached past her to pick up his mobile, which he slapped into her hand.

'What's this for?' she asked, puzzled and annoyed.

'Pizza. Order it. You can pay, since you fed my steak to the crabs. And no girly stuff like capers and asparagus!'

The past week of living with Rowan had been like living within a twister, Seb decided as he strolled into the kitchen. He'd had a tough day at work and his kitchen held Patch, an attractive blonde around Patch's age and Rowan, and they were all stuffing brightly coloured bags with sweets.

'Seb, do you know where I can hire a boat?' Rowan demanded.

'Hello to you too,' Seb said pointedly, and looked at Annie, his face quizzical.

'Seb, this is Annie—my friend. She hired me to organise the party last weekend. Annie, this is Seb, Patch's son,' Rowan gabbled, grabbing a handful of sour worms.

'Hi, Annie. Speaking of that party, the paddock poles still have paint splotches on them,' Seb pointed out.

'I'll get to it. Now, do you know where I can hire a boat?'

'A Hobie? A catamaran? An ocean liner?' Seb asked as he shook hands with Annie. He took the beer Rowan pulled from the fridge for him and twisted off the top.

Rowan wrinkled her nose. 'Something that can accommodate ten teenage girls for a sunset cruise around the harbour.'

Seb, who thought he had a reasonably fast mind, was battling to keep up. 'What are you talking about, Brat?'

Rowan sent him a try-to-keep-up look. 'I had an enquiry about a boat party: food, drink, sunset cruise. I need a boat.'

Seb took a long sip of his beer and rested the neck between his eyes. 'Was she always this exhausting?' he asked Patch.

'Pretty much. Rowan has always only had two speeds: fast and super-fast,' Patch replied, sliding a look at Annie.

Annie smiled slowly, dropped her eyes and lifted them again in a look that was all seduction. Oh, wow, Patch was flirting with a woman his own age. *His own age!*

Seb felt like looking out of the window to see if a pig was flying past. He leaned against the far counter and crossed his legs at the ankles. 'And these bags are for another party you're organising?'

'Yep, for tomorrow.' Rowan flashed him a grin. 'Not here, though. The mummy wanted it at her house, but she didn't want to take the time out from her business to organise the details. So she's paying me an insane amount to set out snacks, organise a magician and a Slip and Slide and to make party bags.' Rowan looked at her watch. 'And Patch and Annie are helping me because I need to get to the bar later.'

As he'd said—a twister. He'd barely seen her this past week. She'd dashed in and out of the house like a woman possessed. He'd tried to get her to stop for a glass of wine, a meal, a conversation. She'd brushed him off, saying that she didn't have time to do anything, and it had annoyed the crap out of him. He'd never been put in the position of running after someone, waiting for someone to give him a minute of their time, and it wasn't fun. Was this how his previous girlfriends felt? Was this a touch of karma?

Karma? Jeez, he sounded like a hippy girl... *Get a grip, dude! You're just freakin' miserable and, frankly, ticked off because you're horny.*

He switched gears fast. 'And your netsukes? Have you done any research yet?'

Rowan pulled a face. 'Not really. I've been so busy...'

'You have a shedload of money tied up in those statues and you're messing around with children's parties?'

Rowan's shoulders stiffened as she sent him a cool look. 'I thought that if I could earn some money I could get back to London and take them to the experts there. That would save me the hassle of trawling the net.'

The reluctance in her voice as she said 'trawling the net' had him shaking his head. 'You don't know where to start, do you?'

Rowan wouldn't meet his eyes. 'Not really.'

'And you couldn't ask me for help? Ro, what do I do for a living?'

Annie's and Patch's eyes played ping-pong as they bounced off their faces.

'It's just that you are busy...'

'That's an asinine excuse! You just didn't want to ask for help—again! I thought we'd talked about your stupid independent streak?'

Rowan launched a sweet at his chest. 'Don't you dare call me stupid!'

Seb snatched the sweet out of the air. 'I never said you were stupid. I said you had a stupid independent streak!'

Patch sighed and looked at Annie. 'I feel like I've been transported back to their childhood. This could go on for a while, so what do you say to leaving them to argue and coming to have a glass of wine at my place?'

And that reminded him… When was his father going to move out of the cottage and back into his own house? Seb opened his mouth to ask, then snapped it closed again. Finish one argument first.

He waited for Patch and Annie to leave—Patch's hand was very low on Annie's back…definitely something happening there—and then banged his bottle down on the counter. He looked at Rowan, who was still packing bags, and rubbed his hands across his face. It annoyed the pants off him that she was living in his house and yet he hardly saw her, that she was so damn close—across the hall from him—yet might as well be in China in terms of being available. He wanted to spend time with her, get to know her, but she was never in the bloody building!

And that felt strange—very bizarre. He'd never actively wanted to seek out a woman's company before, had never wanted to deepen the connection between him and his lovers.

Yet here he was, wanting to spend time with a woman he wasn't sleeping with. It didn't make any sense.

Look at her, Seb thought. Sexiness on steroids. She wore her hair up in a high ponytail and a tank top revealed the curves of the tops of her breasts. It skimmed her long, slim torso and ended an inch above the waistband of her white cotton shorts. Endless slim legs ended in bare feet tipped with fire-red nails. Rowan turned away, bent over to pick up a sweet that had fallen to the floor, and he saw the thin string of the top of her thong, a little red heart on the cross of the white T.

His saliva disappeared as his eyes slid over the rounded

curve of her ass, the knobs of her spine under that thin shirt. The band of her bra, the slim column of her neck.

He took two steps to reach her, and his arm banded around her waist as he hauled her back against him, his hand low on her stomach, pushing her into his throbbing erection.

Rowan spun round and her hips slammed into his. Her eyes were on his mouth as her hands went up to his neck and she mashed her chest against his. Then her mouth slammed against his and she yanked him into a kiss that set his blood on fire.

Rowan was poised for a moment on the edge of that precipice and then she tumbled into kissing Seb. She'd been thinking of this, dreaming about being in his arms again, all week—a mess of sexual frustration—and she'd kept herself super-busy to keep her mind off jumping him again. But now, as his hand grabbed her butt and yanked her up and into him, she could indulge in her need to rediscover those strong muscles, the heat of his skin, his talented hands, his sexy mouth.

Rowan yanked at his shirt and pulled it up his chest, her lips kissing the skin it revealed. Seb pulled the shirt over his head with one hand and Rowan placed her lips on the edge of the fabulous geometric tattoo that covered his shoulder and his bicep.

'I love this,' she murmured against his inked skin. 'So hot, so sexy.'

'I love the way you smell,' Seb replied, his words blowing warm air against her neck. 'Of sunshine and flowers.'

The tip of Rowan's tongue swirled against his collarbone. 'I thought we weren't going to do this…that we were going to get to know each other.'

'I know that you are a brat and that you kiss like a dream,' Seb replied, his hand curling around her breast and his thumb swiping her nipple. 'So I'm good, knowledge-wise, for now.'

Rowan's breath caught in her throat. 'And I know that nobody spikes my temper like you do and that you make my blood boil when you touch me like that. That's all I need to know right now.'

'Bed?' Seb demanded, clasping her face in his hands.

Rowan licked her lips. 'Bed, couch, floor. Take your pick.'

Seb grinned. 'I really like the way you think.'

CHAPTER SEVEN

'ONE OF THESE days we are going to have a post-coital conversation,' Seb muttered as Rowan bounded from his bed and headed into his *en-suite* bathroom.

She grinned as she shoved her hand into the shower and flipped on the taps to boiling. She popped her head around the doorway and smiled again. Seb lay face down on the bed, his head turned in her direction. 'Poor baby, are you feeling neglected?' she teased. 'Do you need me to act like your girlfriend?'

His eyes narrowed. 'I've never needed my actual girlfriends to act like my girlfriend so…no. You're exhausting. You never stay still for a second.'

He was right. She didn't. Staying still gave her too much time to think about things she'd rather not think about—needs that had gone unrecognised for far too long. Like affection and friendship, a sense of belonging, a house to come home to. Since they were too high a price to pay for losing her freedom she pushed them away and refused to think about them.

'One of these days I'm going to tie you to this bed with silk scarves and keep you here.'

Rowan flushed at the thought of being at his mercy, being under his control. Instead of making her feel panicky she felt excitement and…lust. Excitement? Good grief.

But she'd ignore the silk scarves portion of that sentence for a minute...

'Does that mean that you want us to carry on sleeping together?' Rowan demanded, ignoring the pounding shower.

'Since I spend so much time thinking about sleeping with you I might as well just have sex with you.'

'Ooh, don't stop. I just love it when you say such sexy, sweet things,' Rowan drawled.

Seb winced, turned over, and pushed himself up on his elbows. 'Sorry, that sounded churlish.'

Rowan folded her arms against the towel she'd wrapped around her torso. 'Churlish is the least of it.'

Seb rubbed his hand over his head and scowled. 'Dammit, Ro...this situation is going to bite me—us—in the butt, yet I can't stop wanting you. Sleep with you...don't sleep with you. Either way my ass is on the line to get chomped. I look at you and my control flies out of the window.'

Seb had looked as if he was passing a kidney stone as he'd said that, Rowan thought on an internal hiccupped laugh. Still, he was trying to express himself and she appreciated the effort, even if it was clumsy and ass-related. And, really, didn't she feel exactly the same way? She was leaving soon, and had no intention of letting Seb get under her skin, yet here she was, newborn-naked in his room, wishing he'd get out of bed and join her in the shower. And if they did this—continued to sleep together—they had to be very careful about what they were jumping into.

'If we're going to do this then we need to be very sure of what we are doing.' Rowan repeated her thought. 'I'll lay my cards on the table... I like you, and I love sleeping with you, but I *am* going to leave.'

Seb nodded, his gorgeous eyes holding hers. 'I *love* sleeping with you, I like you, and I don't want you to stay.'

Why did that sting? Rowan asked herself. It shouldn't—

couldn't. He was saying what she wanted him to say! Stupid, stupid girl…

'But…'

Rowan tipped her head at his hard tone, his intractable face.

'While we *are* sleeping together we're together. There's only me and you. No one else. No colouring outside the lines.'

She could live with that—wouldn't actually accept anything else. Rowan pushed her shoulders back and tossed her hair. 'Just so you know, I won't act like your girlfriend.'

'Good. I won't act like yours…boyfriend, that is.' Seb pulled a face. 'That's such a juvenile term. How come the word boyfriend sounds so much worse than girlfriend?'

'It's a moot point, since we're not either,' Rowan said firmly as Seb swung his legs off the bed, stood up and walked over to her, all long, lean, masculine grace.

'What time will you be home from your shift at the bar?' he asked, running a possessive hand down her arm.

'My shift ends at twelve. So around half past twelve,' Rowan replied as he put his hands on her hips and backed her into the steaming shower.

He bent his head to her breast and tongued her nipple.

'That sounded remarkably like a question a boyfriend would ask, Hollis,' Rowan said, streaking her hands over his broad shoulders.

Seb picked up his head and sent her a wicked look that had her toes curling.

'Nope, just trying to work out how much time I have to buy some more condoms.' A foil packet appeared as if by magic between his thumb and finger. 'This is the last one. Shower sex?'

Rowan sighed. She was definitely going to have to buy herself a toy when she left… Then she'd be able to drift back to memories of what Seb was doing to her. And why did that thought make her feel instinctively sad?

'Ro?' Seb lifted his head and his hand stilled on her breast. 'You okay to go again?'

She needed to make as many memories as she could. 'Yes, please.'

It was past three in the morning when Rowan parked her car—Yas's car—in the carport next to the three-car garage. Seb's hog sat in one spot, Patch's Jag in the other and his SUV in the last space. Poor little car, Rowan thought, left out in the cold. She glanced up at the house and saw that the light was off in Seb's room. Rowan considered slipping quietly into bed with him, snuggling down for the night, with his back warm against her chest, her legs tucked in behind his knees. And if he woke up so much the better…

No! Rowan shook her head. That would be a girlfriendy thing to do, and she wasn't going to act like that. She and Seb were having sex, for a defined period, then she was leaving and he was staying. Getting cosy was a sure way to get her heart involved, and that would be a disaster of magnificent proportions! Leaving would be so much harder than it needed to be, and settling back into her transient life would take more effort than normal.

Was that why she'd accepted the offer from a couple of the pub's regulars to accompany them into the city and listen to a blues band in a late-night café? Because it was an impulsive decision? Because it was something that she'd do if she was on her own…accept a random invitation from strangers to try something different?

She sometimes felt that she was too comfortable in Seb's house—in his bed, his arms.

She couldn't afford to get too attached to him, to his house or this city, Rowan told herself as she climbed out of the car and headed towards the front door. She had a little over a ten days left here; her parents were due back at the end of next week and she'd spend the weekend with them. Hopefully, if she could land the boat party gig, she'd have enough money to feed and house herself when she got back to London.

Of course if she actually did some work researching those netsukes she could be out of here sooner. She knew Grayson wanted them, and she suspected that, judging by his increasingly frequent e-mails on the subject, and as long as she could prove that they weren't stolen, he might buy them unseen. At the very least she'd recover the cash she'd laid out and then she could go anywhere she wanted to...

She should start with researching the Laughing Buddha—the miniature she'd spotted first in the shop, instantly recognising that it was the stand-out piece of the collection—so why wasn't she carving out some time to research the wretched thing? Sure, it would take a bite out of her money-collecting time, but she wasn't a total numpty on the computer, as she'd made herself out to be to Seb.

Did she want to keep it? Or could it be—dammit—because she was feeling slightly sentimental? A tad grateful to that tiny little object that it had been the catalyst to her coming home?

Home. There—she'd said it. And it was time she acknowledged that, no matter what had transpired before, this *was* home. This house,—*not* the house next door... *This* was home.

Whoomph!

Rowan let out a high-pitched squeal and cannoned into a hard shape as she pushed open the door to Awelfor. Familiar arms grabbed her before she toppled over and her heart steadied as she realised that she'd run into Seb.

'You scared my breath out of me!' She wheezed as she placed a hand on her chest. 'Jeez, Seb!'

Seb flicked on the hall light and Rowan blinked at the

brightness. When the black dots receded she turned to Seb, and her smile faded when she saw that he was dressed in jeans and an old T-shirt and held his car keys in his hands.

'Where are you going at three in morning?' she asked, puzzled.

'To bloody look for you!'

Rowan took a step back as his roar washed over her. Then she saw his wild eyes, his dishevelled hair and his inside-out T-shirt. He was in a complete tizzy and it was fairly obvious that *she* was the cause of it.

'You said that you would be home around half-twelve!' Seb paced the hallway, tension bunching every muscle in his body. 'At twelve-forty-five I was worried. At one-fifteen I was concerned enough to call you on your mobile and I've been calling every ten minutes since then. Why don't you bloody well answer your phone?'

Rowan pulled the mobile out of her bag and checked the display. *Oh, yeah...* She'd missed more than a couple of calls...like fifteen.... 'I'd put my mobile on silent...I didn't think to change it back.'

'And doesn't that just explain a whole lot?' Seb shouted. 'You don't *think*, Rowan. Where on earth have you been?'

Crap. She hadn't seen Seb this mad since she'd chirped him about his ex-fiancée. And he'd passed that level of anger five minutes ago. 'I went to a late-night blues café in Simon's Town.'

'You *what*?'

Rowan thought that she saw the chandelier tremble. 'Whoa, hold on a sec! I thought you'd be sleeping—'

'Like I could *sleep* until I knew you were home safely!'

'Seb, the pub is five minutes away.'

'And I expected you home fifteen minutes or so after the pub closed. And I know it closed at one because I called there too!' Seb shoved his hands into his hair. 'I've been imagining you stabbed or raped or driven off the road—'

'Oh, come on, Seb! You're overreacting!' Rowan retorted. When his eyes lightened she knew that she'd made an tactical error. His anger had just deepened and his eyes had gone cold.

'You know, I *get* that you have this free-spirit, answer-to-no-one gig going on, and I know you well enough to choose my battles with you,' Seb said, his voice colder than an Arctic breeze. 'So I'm prepared to let the little things go… But when you roll in at three in the morning, after saying that you'll be home a lot earlier, I get to yell at you!'

'I'm not a child, and you're not allowed to place restrictions on me!' Rowan snapped, going on the defensive because she suspected that she'd crossed a rather big line.

'You keep telling me that you're not a child, but you're acting like one. A responsible, thoughtful grown-up would've picked up the phone and called me, told me not to worry.'

Seb rubbed the back of his neck with his hand. His anger had faded and she could see disappointment and resignation on his face. She could fight anger. The other two were like acid on her soul.

'Rowan, you're free to come and go as you please. I can't and won't ask you to be something you are not. But I do expect you to think, occasionally, about other people. I was worried. I had a right to be. If not as your lover, then as a man who has known you all your life.' Seb twisted his lips. 'And if you can't see that then you are even more screwed up than any of us thought.'

Seb's words hovered in the air as he walked up the stairs and a minute later she heard his bedroom door close. Rowan sank to the third step of the staircase and dropped her head to her knees. He was right and she couldn't run away from it. She had been selfish and thoughtless and she didn't like being either.

Why couldn't people understand—and why couldn't she explain?—that restrictions felt like chains to her? That rules felt like the bars of that long-ago jail cell and that she couldn't trust anyone not to change the rules on her to suit their needs better?

She knew that he had a point—a really valid point. She knew she should apologise, ask for forgiveness for being thoughtless, but the words were stuck in her throat. Why did she feel that if she apologised she would also be apologising for her lifestyle? For being impulsive, freedom-seeking, for being who she was?

She was at fault and she knew that she should admit it— just go up those steps and say sorry. Wake him up if she had to… But saying *I'm sorry* had become incredibly difficult for her. Maybe it was because she hadn't had anybody in her life for so long to say sorry to—or was it because she'd apologised constantly as a child and a teenager for her high spirits and impulsive behaviour? Back then her apology had always been followed by more lectures, more disappointment, more opportunities to throw her indiscretions back in her face.

By seventeen she'd stopped saying sorry—mostly because nobody had heard her any more. They certainly hadn't believed she was remorseful, and no one except for Callie—God, she loved that woman—had ever attempted to understand why she felt the need to push the barriers, to taste, touch, experience life.

Geez, she sounded like a whiny, childish…victim. *Damn*, she sounded like a *victim*? Did she subconsciously see herself that way? As a casualty of her parents' narrow-minded world view, Joe's deception?

Maybe she did.

And she didn't like it.

So, she could sit on these stairs and think about how misunderstood she was, justify why she should brush this incident under the carpet, but then she'd feel guilty and dreadful—especially since it was pure pride standing in the way of her saying sorry.

Seb would probably give her another lecture on thoughtlessness and selfishness, but she was a big girl. She'd take it, say goodnight and go back to her own room. She could do this—she *had* to do this! If only to prove to him that she had grown up…

Rowan dragged herself up the stairs, hesitated outside Seb's door. When she saw the sliver of light under the door she gently knocked. She heard his 'Come in' and when she entered saw that he was in bed, a computer on his knees. His face was blank when he looked at her.

Rowan put her hands behind her back and gripped the doorframe behind her. 'Sorry. That was selfish and thoughtless of me.'

Seb's face remained inscrutable while he closed his computer and placed it on the bedside table. Rowan shifted from foot to foot while she waited for him to say something.

'Okay. Come here.'

Rowan stepped closer to the bed and wondered what else was coming. When he just looked at her, a small smile on his face, she frowned. 'That's it? No more lectures?'

Seb smiled slightly as he pulled the covers back and shifted across the bed. 'Nope. Hop in.'

Rowan plucked at her T-shirt and shook her head. 'Seb, I can't. I smell of beer and booze. I'm exhausted. I'm going to take a shower and head back to my room.'

'Take a shower and head back here,' Seb said.

His face and voice were calm. Steady. God, she loved his steady.

His bed…it was tempting. So tempting. But so…*girl-friendy.* 'I—I shouldn't.'

'You really should. Come on, Ro, the world won't stop

if you simply sleep in the same bed as me. Besides, I never got to buy those condoms, so you're safe from me…tonight.'

Those eyes were dreamy again. That hard body was relaxed, his face sleepy. He was as tired as she was and she knew that it would now take a cattle prod to get her to go back to her room. 'Okay, I'll just take a quick shower.'

'Mmm, okay. Hurry up,' Seb murmured, his head on the pillow and his eyes closed.

Rowan kept his sleepy face in her mind as she rushed through the shower and brushing her teeth. When she came back into the room, dressed in the T-shirt Seb had been wearing earlier, he was fast asleep. She slid under the covers next to him and felt his arm slide around her waist. She snapped the light off and Seb snuggled closer. She felt his lips in her hair.

'You scared me, Ro. Don't do it again, okay?' he whispered.

'I'll try not to,' Rowan whispered back into the darkness. And she *would* try—but she couldn't guarantee it.

Five days later it was early morning and Rowan sat in the cushioned area of Seb's bay window. She stared over the hedge to the windows of her old bedroom, with Seb's gentle breathing the soundtrack to her thoughts.

She still hadn't gone home—still hadn't managed to slip through the gate and walk around her mum's prize rose garden, or sit on the bench outside, where her father had always used to read the Sunday papers in the winter sun.

They were due home in less than a week and she still hadn't wrapped her head around how she was going to approach them, deal with them. Should she e-mail them and tell them that she was home and staying with Seb? Should she just wait and rock up on their doorstep? How would they react? What would they say, feel, want from her?

Would they be able to see her as a grown woman who

made her own decisions and lived with the consequences thereof? Would she receive any respect from them for doing that? Any understanding? She no longer required them to be supportive of her, of her lifestyle, but she didn't want to listen to them nag her about settling down, studying further, about her clothes and her hair and her inability to make good choices...

Seb rolled over in his sleep and Rowan watched him for a moment. How would her parents react when they found out about her and Seb? Because find out they would. They weren't completely oblivious to everything around them, and she and Seb gave off enough heat to generate a nuclear reaction. They wouldn't understand the concept of a short-term, mutually satisfying sexual relationship. They'd been childhood sweethearts and hadn't, as far as she knew—and she probably didn't, because her parents were about as talkative as clams—dated anyone else.

They'd probably worry more about Seb than they would about her. Seb was a part of their lives, a constant presence, while she was their erratic and eccentric wayward daughter.

'Ro? You okay?' Seb asked from his massive double bed, leaning back on his elbows, his hair rumpled from sleep.

Gorgeous man, Rowan thought.

'Mmm, just wrapping my head around visiting the old house.'

'You still haven't been over?'

Rowan shrugged. 'I really should. It's funny—funny ironic, not ha-ha—that I can walk into a slum in Bombay or a yurt in Mongolia but I haven't managed to screw up the courage to go home. Every time I think about going over I feel like I'm eighteen again. Lost, alone, scared. I don't like feeling like that, Seb.'

'Understandable. Want me to go with you?' Seb asked, sitting up and crossing his legs. 'And then if you feel like you're eighteen you can tell me and I'll kiss you, or touch you, and remind you that you're all woman.'

'Generous of you.' How did he always manage to make her smile when she was feeling blue? Rowan bundled her hair up, held it on top of her head for thirty seconds before allowing it to fall again.

'Okay, we'll go over later. Tell me about your travelling.'

Rowan turned to face him, her back to the window. 'That's a pretty broad subject. Narrow it down…'

Seb thought for a moment. 'Tell me what you love about travelling.'

'The colour, the wonderful local people, their tolerance; the differences that are wonderful, the similarities that are universal. Buildings, bazaars, street food.'

'And what do you most hate about it?'

'Practically? Dirty kitchens and cheap hostel dorm rooms. The constant partying all around. The same questions all the time. "Where do you come from?" "How much of the world have you seen?" "How long have you been travelling for?" "Where to next?" Boring conversations, over and over and over again…' Rowan hesitated.

'Tell me, Ro.'

Rowan gestured to the bed. 'This…'

'This?' Seb looked puzzled. He looked at the bed and then turned his gaze back to hers. 'What?'

'One of the worst things about travelling is relationships: finding them, keeping them, losing them. I have said goodbye far too many times, Seb. Far more than any person should. Ever. I can go for weeks without meeting another traveller, depending on where I'm staying, because I don't want to…don't want to get to know them and then have to wave them off.'

'Are we talking about friendships or lovers?'

'Either. Both,' Rowan said. 'Saying goodbye always hurts.'

And it will hurt so much more when I have to say goodbye to you, Rowan thought, holding his intense gaze. She knew from talking to other backpackers and from her couple of failed relationships that a relationship limited by time, like hers and Seb's, was always more passionate than a normal, run-of-the-mill romance in the real world. They both knew that it had to end some time soon, so they had to make every moment count.

It wasn't real. Or maybe it was too real. It just wasn't built to last.

It would end with another goodbye. And she already knew that it would be absolutely the hardest goodbye she'd ever have to say.

Seb ran his hand through his very short hair and then over his stubbled jaw. He looked as if he wanted to say something, pursue the subject, but then she saw him retreat. Was he running from the emotion in her voice? From the sentimentality of her words? She knew that he'd never been good at dealing with raw emotion. He preferred to find a rational explanation behind every decision or action. She envied him that ability to be so clear-thinking, so sensible.

She couldn't be like that... She felt everything. Twice.

'Oh, hey...I've been meaning to ask you. Do you want to come with me to a cocktail party tomorrow night? It would be nice to go with someone.'

Rowan blinked at the change of subject, thought for a moment, and then said, 'I'd love to, but I don't have anything that could even vaguely pass as a cocktail dress.' She held up her hand to stop Seb from talking. 'And, no, you are *not* going to buy me a dress and shoes for one evening! What a waste! So, sorry—no can do.'

'Oh, come on, Ro. It's just money.' Seb rolled out of bed and walked over to her, his sleeping shorts riding low on his hips. He bent down, brushed his lips across hers and pulled her to her feet.

'It's money I would have to pay you back. I'm already in debt to you for the airfare from Jo'burg to here, for the airfare when I leave—though maybe I might be able to pay for some of that...'

'Then get your ass onto a computer and do something about your netsukes,' Seb complained, his hands loose on her hips. He looked down at her, assessing her. 'I have a feeling that you don't want to sell them.'

Rowan wrinkled her nose, thought about denying it and shrugged. 'I really don't want to sell the Laughing Buddha. But I have to sell the others. I can't afford a twelve-thousand-pound indulgence—especially when I owe you money.'

Seb rested his forehead against hers. 'I can understand why you want to keep it. It's stunning. As for owing me money...it's not important.'

Rowan stroked the side of his neck. 'It's important to me. I can't take your money, Seb.'

'You could give lessons in stubborn to mules, Brat,' Seb muttered.

'I know...' Rowan dug her fingers into the light smattering of his chest hair. 'Listen, are those massive chests still up in the attic?'

'As far as I know.' Seb sat back, looking puzzled at her change of subject. 'Why?'

'Callie and I used to play dress-up with your grandmother's dresses. If I remember right she was quite a socialite in her day.'

Seb—smart guy—immediately made the connection.

'Ro, you cannot possibly wear a sixty, seventy-year-old dress! Fish moths! Dust!'

'Dry cleaners! And Yas banished fish moths a hundred years ago. Haven't you ever heard of vintage dresses? I think there were shoes up there too.'

'You're nuts.'

Rowan raised an eyebrow. 'Do you want me to go with you or not?'

'Oh, okay. We'll take a look. If we don't find anything, then I'll buy you a dress and no arguments—okay?'

'Maybe.'

Seb kissed her nose. 'So, plan of action for the day… Sex, breakfast, a quick visit to the War Room for me, a tour of your old place for both of us and then up to the attic. Then sex again. And then sex later.'

'And maybe sex for pudding,' Rowan said dryly.

Seb laughed. 'You catch on quick.'

Limited time, maximum pleasure, Rowan thought as he swept her into a kiss that had her toes curling. And, yeah, saying goodbye to him was going to sting.

CHAPTER EIGHT

SEB, NOT FINDING Rowan in any of the rooms downstairs, jogged up the stairs to the main floor. Instead of turning left, as he usually did, he took the second flight set of stairs, passing the closed doors to the smaller rooms that hadn't been used since his grandparents' day—such a waste of space—and heading for the narrow stairs that led up to the attic.

He wondered when last he'd been up here. Fifteen, twenty years? Callie and Rowan had used to play up here all the time when he'd been glued to his computer.

Some things never changed, he thought sourly. He'd planned to spend most of this day with Ro, but his staff had run into sophisticated firewalls on a site they needed to crack—today—and it had taken all their combined strategy skills to climb over, under and around them. As a result he'd spent most of the day in the War Room and hadn't seen Ro since breakfast.

He wondered if she'd gone next door, but doubted it.

Seb poked his head into the attic and looked around. Instead of being dark and poky the attic was filled with natural light, courtesy of the skylights in the roof. The usual detritus filled the space directly in front of him—boxes that were labelled 'Christmas decorations', old computers, a set of water skis, and a pile of life jackets lay on top of more stacked cardboard boxes.

He really needed to toss some of this rubbish out.

'Ro?'

'To your left, Seb,' Rowan called.

Seb turned and followed her voice, walking around a wooden partition, and blinked in surprise. Thick, old-fashioned oak chests spilled garments over the rough blankets Rowan had placed on the floor, and in the centre of the clothes-spill Rowan stood in front of an antique full-length mirror framed in oak, dressed in a sleek black gown and three-inch heels. Even with her hair in a messy ponytail and a make-up-free face she looked stunning.

'What do you think?'

'That's a hell of a dress. Did you spray paint it on?'

'Ha-ha. Your gran was slightly skinnier than I am.'

His grandmother... He'd never known her, but he'd like to know how anyone could have so many clothes. He stepped over a pile of coats and looked down at the garments closest to his feet. Jeans, a thigh-length leather jacket, a velvet trenchcoat, a white linen suit.

'These are too modern to be my grandmother's clothes.'

'I think they're your mum's—what she left behind. There are a couple of nice dresses... Do you mind?'

Seb felt his throat clench and forced himself to shrug carelessly. 'Knock yourself out. She left them here, didn't she?'

Rowan looked at him with sympathetic eyes and he hoped that she wouldn't say anything. He didn't discuss his mother—ever. The longest discussion he'd had about her had been with his father a week or so ago.

Rowan ran her hands over her hips and turned back to the mirror. 'What do you think of this dress?'

Seb looked at her properly, felt the saliva disappearing from his mouth and swallowed several times. Hot, hot, *hot*. He couldn't find the words...

'Uh...' he grunted as his brain shut down.

Rowan looked at her reflection and tipped her head. 'You're right. I never liked this shade of black.'

How could she possibly take his silence to mean that he didn't like the dress? Was she mad? It was figure-hugging, cleavage-revealing, backless and strapless.

It sent every blood corpuscle heading south.

Seb smacked the ball of his hand against his temple to reboot his speech function. 'I love the dress, And black is black…isn't it?'

Rowan sent him a pitying look. The kind women reserved for those moments when they thought men had the understanding of a two-year-old. 'Of course there are shades of black. Obsidian, peppercorn, domino, raven, ebony…'

Seb felt as if he'd fallen into an alternative universe. 'Peppercorn is a shade of black?'

'There are many shades of red—fire engine, cherry, scarlet—why can't there be shades of black?'

'I have no idea what you're talking about. And I really don't care.' *All I want to do is get you out of that dress.* To distract himself from that thought, he looked around again. 'Good God, look at these clothes! I never knew there was so much still up here.'

Rowan's eyes were shining with pleasure. 'They're fabulous. I've seen six cocktail dresses I want to try on.'

'I like that one you have on,' Seb said gruffly. 'Wear that.'

Rowan shook her head. 'This is a ballgown—too much for a cocktail party. I just couldn't resist trying it on.'

'Aren't they out of fashion?' Seb asked, toeing a froth of purple silk.

'Designer dresses like these are never out of fashion.' Rowan disappeared behind a screen in the corner. 'And it seems like your gran's taste ran to classic, timeless outfits.'

Good for Gran, Seb thought as he walked to the centre

of the room and sat on the dusty floor, crossing his legs at the ankles.

'What do you think?'

Seb glanced up and swallowed his tongue. The dress was red, a shocking slap to the senses, low-cut, and with what seemed like a million tassels falling to just under her backside. 'It's red. And short.'

'It's raspberry, and I'm decent underneath.'

Rowan twirled, the tassels whirled, and Seb saw the high-cut shorts underneath in the same shade.

'It's a heart attack dress,' Seb said. 'A bit too much for a corporate do.'

Rowan looked at herself in the mirror. 'Mmm, maybe you're right.'

Seb removed his smartphone from the back pocket of his jeans and checked his e-mails while Rowan changed again. Why she had to disappear each time to change was a puzzle for another day. He'd seen—and tasted—every inch of her, quite a few times.

'Ready for the next one?' Rowan asked cheerfully.

Seb grinned. 'Hit me.'

Seb leaned back on his elbow and almost choked at the puffball that sashayed across the wooden floor. It was orange, it was ruffled, and it was hideous. He searched for something to say and decided that no words could describe the awfulness of the dress.

'That bad, huh?' Rowan arched an eyebrow, turned to look in the mirror and laughed. 'Oh, *yuk*! I look like orange icing.'

Seb laughed. 'I think the proper shade is cosmic carrot. Take it off, please, and we'll burn it!'

'Not a bad idea,' Rowan agreed.

Seb watched as the gown got thrown out towards the chest and imagined her next to naked behind that screen. It

took all his will-power to stay where he was, and the front
of his jeans was growing tighter by the second.

The next three dresses were all black, sexy and sophisticated. Seb used the orange monstrosity for a pillow and
spread out on the floor, lazy in the diffused sunlight that
drifted through the skylights. He could think of worse ways
to spend a lazy late afternoon than watching a sexy woman
model slinky dresses for him.

'This is it,' Rowan declared. 'If this one isn't suitable,
then I give up. I want a glass of wine.'

'Let's see it.'

Seb turned his head and his heart bumped in his chest.
He slowly sat up and looked at Rowan, who was looking
at herself in the mirror. The dress was a colour somewhere
between blue and silver, low-cut, and a concoction of lace
and fine ruffles. He could see glimpses of her fine skin
through the lace and his saliva disappeared.

He remembered that dress—remembered his mother
wearing it to a party some time shortly before she'd left
for good. She'd grabbed him as she walked out through the
door, pulling his reluctant twelve-year-old self into a hug
that he'd professed to hate and secretly adored.

Mostly because her hugs had been so rare and infrequent. Laura had not been affectionate or spontaneous, and
gestures like those were imprinted on his memory. She'd
smelled of vanilla and she'd worn her blonde hair piled up
onto her head.

Two weeks after wearing that dress out she'd been gone.
For ever.

'I love this…love the lace…' Rowan bubbled, turning
in front of the mirror.

When he didn't respond, she turned to look at him. She
crouched down in front of him, her cool hands on his face.

'Seb? What's wrong?'

Seb tried to shake off his sadness. The hurt that he normally kept so deeply buried was frying his soul. He attempted a smile but knew that it didn't come close.

'Please, please talk to me,' Rowan begged.

Seb reached out and touched the fabric that draped her knees. 'This was my mum's.'

'Oh, sweetie. I'm sorry.' Rowan rested her head on his. 'I'll take it off, find something else to wear.'

'Actually, it's a happy memory. I remember her wearing it just before she left. She hugged me, called me her computer geek, said something about…' He tried to recall her exact words but they were lost in time. 'Um, how someone like her had managed to produce someone as bright as me. Or something like that.'

'I remember her vaguely.'

'So does Callie. You were—what?—seven when she left?'

'I was seven. Cal was six.' Rowan pulled the dress above her knees and sat down on the blanket next to Seb.

'I still feel crap that Callie didn't have a mother growing up.'

'Neither did you, Seb. Cal didn't feel the effects of her leaving as much as you did, sweetie. She had Yas,,,we both had Yas. My mother was so involved in Peter's life and his studies and her music that she didn't have much energy or time left over for me. So when we needed a hug, comfort, or to talk to someone we turned to each other or to Yas. Grumpy, spinsterish, with a tongue that can slice metal. It's strange without her here in Awelfor.'

Seb ran his hand down her calf, knowing that she was trying to lighten his mood. 'If she was here you wouldn't be sleeping in my bed.'

Rowan laughed and quoted one of Yasmeen's favourite expressions. '"You want the milk, buy the cow!"'

Seb grinned, and then his smile faded as he looked at the dress again. He was silent for a long time before stating quietly, 'She's in Brazil, in Salvador. Low on funds. She was in the hospital a couple of months ago with a burst appendix.'

Why had he told her that? Why did he want her to know? This wasn't like him, Seb thought, regretting the words that he'd let fly out of his mouth. He didn't have this type of conversation with the women he was sleeping with—didn't have this type of conversation at all.

What was it about Rowan that made him want to open up to her? To let her see behind the steel-plated armour he'd so carefully constructed? Was it because he'd always known her? Because she was Callie's friend and now his too? Was it those deep black sympathetic eyes that held understanding but no pity?

'When did you find out where she is?'

'I've always known where she is,' Seb said, his voice harsh.

'How?'

Seb lifted his eyebrows at her. 'What do I do for a living, Ro?'

'Oh,' Rowan whispered, connecting the dots.

Seb rubbed the material between his fingers again. 'I found her when I was about sixteen. She was in Prague. I managed to get hold of an e-mail address and I sent her a couple of letters…angry, vicious letters…demanding to know why she'd left and then, in the next breath, begging that she come home.'

'Did she ever reply?'

Seb shook his head. 'She changed her e-mail address and I lost track of her for a while. I'd tell myself that I didn't give a damn and wouldn't look for her. Then something would happen and I'd start again. But I never sent her another e-mail. I just need to know…you know…that she's alive. And okay. Not in trouble…'

'But you send her money.'

Seb's eyes flew up to meet hers and Rowan shook her head at him.

'You do send her money. Oh, Seb, you...'

'Sucker? Chump? Idiot?'

Rowan placed her fingers over his lips. 'You're putting words into my mouth. I was going to say you shouldn't.'

He felt his cheeks flush. 'She's often broke. What can I do? It's just money. I don't know why everyone gets all heated up about it. Money is easy...'

Rowan nodded her head. It was. Of course it was. To him. Money was black and white, no shades of grey, clearly defined. It held no emotion, no grudge, didn't waver or prevaricate. He understood money. People, with all their flaws and craziness and ups and downs, flummoxed him.

'What am I supposed to do, Ro? Not send her cash? Let her suffer because we suffered?' he demanded.

Rowan saw the decades of pain buried deep and bit back her protective response—the one that made her want to snap, *Yeah! You should let her climb out of the hole she's dug herself into!* Instead she bit her tongue and knew that he needed to talk to her, to someone, about his mum. Even tough guys, seemingly unemotional guys, needed to unload occasionally.

Rowan suspected that Seb was long overdue.

'How many times have you sent money?' she asked in her most neutral voice.

'A couple of times a year for the past few years,' Seb admitted reluctantly. 'Before that she seemed to be okay for funds.'

'And, if I know you, you probably sent a lump sum every time?'

'It was always an anonymous deposit. There is no way she can trace who it came from.'

Rowan sucked in her cheeks and gazed at the floor, literally swallowing the angry words at the back of her throat.

His mother was many things, but she wasn't stupid, and she had to at the very least suspect that it was Seb. How many people would she have met and had a big enough impact on for them to make anonymous, generous ongoing deposits into her bank account? Who else would it be other than her computer genius son? And she'd never sent him an e-mail to say thank you, to acknowledge him...

Oooh, that was rough.

Rowan looked down at her hands, vibrating with tension. Good grief, families were complicated. Parent-child relationships could be crazy. The ways to mess up your children were infinite, she decided.

Seb still held the hem of her dress—his mum's dress—between his fingers and Rowan looked at his bent head, at the masculine planes of his face, the tiny tick of tension in that single dimple in his cheek. Her tough guy, smart guy, good guy. So strong, so alpha, so damn attractive in his complexity. She'd known him for ever but she felt that she could spend another lifetime discovering all the nuances of his personality; he was that layered, that interesting.

That intriguing.

Ugh, pull up those reins, cowgirl. Your horse is bolting away from you... You're not going to get sappy and sentimental. You can't afford to, and you know this!

Rowan stood up, grabbed the edges of the hem of the dress and pulled it up and over her head. Seb gaped as she stood in front of him in just a brief pair of white panties and silver heels. No bra.

His eyes clouded over and Rowan smiled a tiny smile of feminine satisfaction. So sue her. She could make this hot guy salivate, and as a bonus banish the sadness from his eyes.

She looked at the dress in her hand. 'I love this dress... but I understand if you don't want me to wear it.'

Seb bit the inside of his lip. 'I want to say yes but…
Maybe some day. Just…'

'Not today.' Rowan nodded her understanding. She
looked at the pile of discarded dresses on the floor. 'Okay,
black it is, then. Which one?'

Seb pulled a face. 'Ugh. Come on, Ro, let me take you
shopping. One dress, one pair of shoes… Consider it as
nine years' worth of Christmas and birthday presents I
never got to buy.'

He needs to do this, Rowan realised. *He needs to spoil
me—wants to do something for me that is outside of the
crazy little deals we've struck to work around my pride and
independence.* Could she allow him to do that, or would
her stiff neck and habitual self-reliance spoil it for him?

It was hard. She couldn't lie. But seeing the pleasure
on his face when she finally nodded her agreement was
worth the risk.

He scooted up, dropped a kiss on her nose and grabbed
her hand. 'Okay, let's go. Now.'

'Good grief, Hollis, I'm still half naked!' Rowan protested. 'Pass me my clothes, Einstein.'

Seb picked up her pink T-shirt from the floor next to his
foot and Rowan saw that he did it with great reluctance.
His eyes were firmly on her breasts.

She grabbed his chin and forced him to look in her eyes.
'Get your head out of bed, Seb. We're going shopping. For
a dress. And shoes. Cocktail dresses and shoes are expensive, by the way.'

Seb grinned. 'I'm pretty sure my credit card can stand it.'

Rowan let him go, stepped away and picked up her
shorts. She pulled them up, zipped, and placed her hands
on her hips. 'Seb?'

'Yeah?'

'Your mum's failings are hers, not yours. You didn't do

or say anything that made her leave. That was on her and not on you.'

Seb pulled her close and buried his face in her hair. Just stood with her in his arms. She didn't know where those words had come from. She just knew, soul-deep, that he'd needed to hear them.

Just as she knew that all she had to do right then was hold him.

And when he pulled away to let go she pretended that the moment *hadn't* been charged with all those pesky emotions he tried so damn hard to ignore.

She did it because quite simply he needed her to.

'I need an ice cream,' Seb whined theatrically, and Rowan rolled her eyes at him.

What a lightweight, she thought. They'd only done one level of the mall and there were three more to go. She still hadn't found a dress that was both within the budget she'd set in her head—she didn't care how flexible Seb's credit card was; she was *not* going to pay a fortune for a dress she'd only wear once!—and nice enough to wear.

'Or a beer. Actually, I definitely need a beer,' Seb added as she pulled him into a tiny boutique that looked interesting.

'This was your idea,' Rowan told him, unsympathetic, and headed for a rail of dresses at the back of the shop.

Black, black, red… She pulled a coral chiffon cocktail dress off a hanger and held it up to look at it. Oh, it was pretty, she admitted as she held it against her and looked in the full-length mirror against the wall. It was sleeveless with a dropped waist and a multi-tiered skirt that fell to mid-thigh.

Take me home, it whispered urgently.

'That's the one,' Seb stated, jamming his hands into the

pockets of his shorts while Rowan looked for a price tag. 'Go try it on.'

No tag, Rowan thought, and knew that it would cost a bomb. She had an eye for picking out quality. She sighed. In clothes and in *objets d'art*.

Rowan shook her head and replaced the hanger on the rail. 'We'll look for something else.'

Seb tugged it off the rail and thrust it at her. 'Try it on.'

'It's the perfect colour for you,' the shop assistant stated, and Rowan narrowed her eyes at her.

'Stop being stubborn and try the bloody thing on.' Seb pushed her towards the discreet dressing room. He turned to the shop assistant. 'Shoes?'

'Silver diamante sandals. I have the perfect pair. Size seven?'

'Of course you do,' Rowan muttered as she stepped into the dressing room. She raised her voice so that it could be heard above the partition. 'Size six.'

Rowan slipped her clothes off, carefully undid the discreet zip and slid the dress over her head. *Yeah, this is the dress,* she thought; it was a pity she couldn't have it.

'Does it fit?' Seb demanded.

'Yes. Beautifully. It's a fairytale dress.'

And she was living in a fairytale at the moment. She had the run of a gorgeous house she'd always loved and was sleeping with a super-hot, sometimes not-so-charming prince.

She was loving every second of it.

But it wasn't real life, Rowan reminded herself. She—no, they were *both* enthralled by their sexual chemistry, and it was colouring how they saw each other. When the dust settled, they'd start to argue, and then they'd start to fight, and soon—as per usual—they wouldn't be able to stand each other.

Because the best predictor of future behaviour was past

behaviour, and neither of them had a very good track record at playing nice for extended periods.

Then why did she feel so settled, living in Seb's house, living with Seb? Was a part of her yearning for the stability of living in one place with one man? At twenty-eight was her biological clock starting to tick? Was it just being in Seb's home, waking up in Seb's arms, that had her wanting to believe that she could be happy with the picket fence and the two point four kids and the Labrador and…?

You're being ridiculous, she told herself. *The grass always looks greener on the other side.* She knew this—heck, she knew this well.

Before coming home she had never had a serious thought about settling down, about relationships and children and suburbia. Okay, that was a lie—of course she had—but only little, non-serious thoughts. Even *she* knew she was capable of being seduced by the idea of *what-if,* of thinking that a wonderful experience could translate into a wonderful life in that place. Hadn't she gone through something similar in Bali, where she'd thought she'd buy a little house and stay for ever? And when she'd first seen the Teton mountain range, and that gorgeous little cake shop that had been for sale in the Cotswolds? She'd imagined herself living and working in all those places, but the urge to move on had always come—as it would here as well.

'Rowan? You lost in there?'

Seb's voice pulled her out of her reverie.

'Coming.' Rowan pulled on her clothes, stepped out of the room and handed the assistant the dress. 'Thanks, but we'll keep looking.'

The assistant looked at Seb, eyebrows raised, as she slipped the dress into an expensive cover.

'I've already paid for it. Shoes too.' Seb took the covered dress, slung it over his shoulder and grabbed the bag holding her shoes. 'Can we please get a beer now?'

'You paid for it?' Rowan asked in a icy voice. 'What on earth...?'

'You said it fitted beautifully, it's your colour, and I could see that you love it,' Seb replied, puzzled. 'I'm not seeing the problem here.'

'The problem is that it costs a fortune!' Rowan grabbed the bag and peered inside at the shoe box. 'And the shoes are *designer*!'

'Geez, you're boring when you rattle on and on about money.' Seb yawned. 'You agreed that I could buy you a dress and shoes. I've bought you a dress and shoes. Can we move on to the next subject for the love of God? Please?'

Rowan sent him a dirty look, turned on her heel and stomped out of the shop. Outplayed and outmanoeuvred, she thought, and she didn't like it.

Yes, he was on-fire hot, and he was really good company, but she had to remember that Seb could be sneaky sharp when he wanted to be.

'Beer... Food...' Seb breathed in her ear, before grabbing her hand, tugging her around and pushing her in the opposite direction. 'The food court is this way.'

CHAPTER NINE

SEB SNAGGED AN outside table belonging to a funky-looking bistro, draped Rowan's dress on the third chair and grinned at her sulky face. She still wasn't happy about the dress... No, she loved the dress, but she didn't like the idea of him buying it for her.

She took independence to stupid heights, he thought. So the dress was expensive? So were his computers and the technology he loved to spend money on.

His last computer had cost him three times what he'd paid for the dress...

'Stop sulking and order a drink,' he told her, and grinned as her pert nose lifted in the air. He smiled up at the red-headed waitress, placed their orders and leaned back in his chair.

'Thank you for the dress,' she said primly, politeness on a knife-edge. 'And the shoes.'

'I can't wait to get you out of it,' he said, just to rattle her cage.

'Your chances of doing so are diminishing rapidly,' Rowan retorted, but her lips twitched with humour. 'Do you really like the dress or did you just want to stop shopping?'

'Both,' Seb admitted, funeral-director-mournful. 'The things you make me do, Brat.'

'Talking of that...' Rowan gestured to the huge electronic advertising board to the left of them. 'I saw a sign advertising an antiques fair and night market in Scarborough tonight. We could go take a look when we're finished eating.'

'Yeah...no. I'd rather eat jellyfish. Besides, I have a houseful of antiques and you're broke.' Seb took the beer the waitress had placed on the table and drained half the glass in one swallow.

'Thanks for reminding me,' Rowan grumbled. 'And I'm not broke. I'm financially constrained. Asset-rich and cash-poor. We don't have to buy—we could just look.'

Seb mimed putting a gun to his head and pulling the trigger and Rowan laughed.

They sat and sipped their drinks in a comfortable silence before Seb asked, 'By the way, what happened to the boat party you were organising?'

'Ah, the sixteen-year-old birthday girl changed her mind. Now she wants to go to a Justin Bieber concert instead.'

Seb shuddered.

'I'm getting party enquiries all the time, but I don't want to take on anything I can't deliver in the next week or so. You said that my parents should be home on Sunday—four days from now—and I have to be in London by the following weekend to meet Grayson, so there's no point in trying to get too involved. Pity, because it's good money.'

'So you'll be gone in a week or so?' Seb asked in a very even voice that hid all the emotion in his voice.

'That's the plan,' Rowan said lightly as her heart contracted violently. A week? Was that all they had? Where had the last two weeks gone? She wanted them back, dammit.

'God...' Seb muttered into his drink.

It would be another goodbye and the hardest one that she'd ever have to say. Harder even than that first one, when she'd run away to find herself, to find out what made sense to her. When had he become so important? So hard to leave?

'Did you go next door this afternoon?' Seb asked, changing the subject.

Rowan nodded.

'And...?'

She shrugged. 'It's just a house. They haven't changed much.'

'Your parents don't do change.'

'But I do, and maybe now I can look at them differently.' Rowan took a sip of wine and looked thoughtful. 'I did a great deal of thinking this afternoon, so maybe it was a good thing that you got tied up at work.'

'I want to hear about it, but maybe we should order first.' Seb beckoned the waitress over, asked for two gourmet burgers and another round of drinks. When the waitress had left, he gestured to Rowan with his glass. 'Talk.'

'How come you just expect me to spill my guts but you don't?'

'Because you're the emotional one and I'm not,' Seb replied.

Except that she was beginning to realise that Seb was far more emotional than anyone knew. He just had years of hiding it.

'I'm starting to think that Fate had a hand in me coming home—that it's telling me that I need to pull my head out of the sand and start dealing with all those old hurts and grievances. If I hadn't bought those netsukes, run out of cash and been flagged by Oz immigration I wouldn't be here.'

'Having amazing sex with your arch enemy?' Seb interjected.

'Having amazing sex with my old friend,' Rowan corrected, and saw the flare of appreciation, of attraction... fondness?...in his eyes. *No emotion, my ass.*

'I need to see my parents, deal with my issues around my mother, reconcile with them—her. Mostly her.' Rowan sighed. 'Maybe I'm finally starting to understand that we are very different people. I wasn't the daughter she needed and she didn't understand what I needed—especially that night I got arrested—but…but my childhood is over. I need to find a new "normal" with them.'

Seb folded his arms and placed them on the table. He linked his fingers in hers and stared down at their hands. 'I never understood why you ran. You were always a fighter. You always came out of the corner ready to fight.'

Rowan nibbled her lip. 'I got knocked down one too many times, resulting in emotional concussion.'

'That's a new one… Who knocked you down?'

'My parents—my mum especially. Peter, Joe Clark…'

'Your dipstick ex? What did he do…exactly? Apart from frame you?'

'When did you realise he had?'

'I think I've probably always known. What else did he do?'

Rowan blew out her breath and held his eye. It was time she told him—time she told someone the whole truth of that evening.

'I fell in love with him. He was kind and sweet and said all the right things to get me into bed. I kept him waiting because…you know…he was my first, and I wanted to make sure he was the right one. Someone who really loved me and not someone who was using me… Ha-ha, what a joke!'

Seb's face hardened. 'So he took your virginity…?'

'Yeah, we made love three hours before we got to the club. The policeman knew the drugs weren't mine—he even admitted it to me—but they were on me and he had to arrest me. Joe told me while he was laughing at me for getting arrested that he'd just wanted to bag and bed "the virgin rebel". That's what he called me.'

Seb swore, low and slow. 'I swear I'm going to rearrange his face.'

'I'm over it—over him. I really am.' Rowan managed a

small smile. 'But it wasn't the best night of my life. I was reeling. I'd had my heart kicked around by the boy who had just taken me to bed—the whole experience of which, sadly, was not nearly as brilliant as I thought it would be—'

'Bad?'

Trust a man to get distracted by sex, Rowan thought as she rocked her hand in the air. 'Meh…'

'Meh?'

'Not good, not bad—and I am *not* discussing my first sexual experience with you, Hollis. Jeez! Do you want to hear this or not?'

'Keep your panties on… So you went off to jail…'

'I had been there for a day or so and I was so scared, terrified. Another young girl had been arrested for something—I can't remember what. Her mother came to the jail, and when they wouldn't release this girl her mother came into the cell with her and just held her until she *could* be released. I wanted that like I've never wanted anything in my life.'

Rowan swallowed and took a deep slug of her wine.

'I just wanted my mother to love me, to support me, to hold me while I sat in that corner. And I knew that she wouldn't. Ever. That hurt more than anything else. So when I got home I thought I would test my theory; how far could I push her until I got a reaction out of her? I never got much of one. My dad screamed and raged and tried to lay down the law but my mum switched off. Until the day I wrote my finals. I came home and she and I had a…discussion.'

'About…?'

Okay, so this was something that she'd never told anybody. Not even Callie. 'My life, my plans. I told her I wanted to go overseas and she immediately agreed. Said it was the first sensible sentence I'd uttered all year.'

'What the…?'

'She said that it would be good for all of us—mainly

her, I think—that I went. I heard the subtext in her speech; she'd had enough of me and her life would be that much easier if I were out of her face. So I packed my stuff, took the money she offered—she was the one who cashed in those unit trusts of my grandmother's—and caught the first plane I could.'

'God, Ro...'

Seb ran his hand over his face and felt sick. They'd all known that Ro and her mum bumped heads, known that Peter was her obvious favourite, but they'd never believed—not for a second—that their relationship had been that broken. Okay, his mother wasn't a saint, and she'd left and it sucked, but she hadn't constantly been there, physically present but emotionally unavailable.

Rowan's staying away from Cape Town made a lot more sense now.

'I'm so sorry,' he muttered, knowing his words were inadequate and stupid after so much time.

But he didn't know what else to say—how to convey how angry and...sad he felt. Because, unlike him, Rowan had needed to be nurtured and shown affection, to be bolstered and boosted. She'd needed affection and love and affirmation.

Bile roiled in his stomach as the waitress placed their burgers in front of them. 'I should take you home...let me take you home.'

Then he felt Rowan's hand cover his, her touch comforting him when he should be comforting her.

'Your mind is going into overdrive, Seb. I'm fine now and I've learnt to live with it. I'm way over Joe Clark and him screwing me—figuratively and literally. As for my mum...she is what she is. I've grown up...'

'But you'd still like a relationship with her?'

'I'd love a relationship with her. So I'll see her, say my sorrys if that's what she needs to hear, and try again.'

He turned and stared down into her face. Oh, dear God, he could fall for her; tumble for this brave, beautiful woman with midnight in her eyes.

Seb shook his head, trying to replace emotion with rational thought. He was just feeling sorry for her, feeling guilty because he hadn't pushed hard enough, dug deep enough to find out the truth about her before this. He'd always known that there was more to Rowan's story, more to Rowan.

Besides she was leaving…*soon*. And he had no intention of letting anyone else leave with his heart again.

Mothers…jeez. The million and two ways they could screw you up.

Rowan popped a chip in her mouth and chewed thoughtfully. 'I really want to go to that antiques market, Seb.'

Seb picked up his knife and fork, looked at his food, and put them down again. He really didn't feel like eating.

'What?' he asked, his mind still reeling. He digested her words, understood them and frowned. 'Are you playing me?' he demanded, innately suspicious of her cajoling face. 'Are you making me feel sorry for you to get what you want?'

Rowan chuckled. 'It's what we woman do. You're smart enough not to fall for it.'

'Brat.'

'Let me try something else.' Rowan batted her eyelashes at him. 'If you take me I'll let you charm me out of that dress.'

Seb looked her up and down and slowly grinned. 'I'm going to charm you out of that dress anyway, so no deal.'

Rowan twisted her lips to hide her grin. 'I *can* resist you, you know.'

Laughter chased the shadows out of Seb's eyes. 'No, you can't. I can't resist you either. Eat—you're going to need the energy.'

'Is that a threat?' Rowan asked silkily.

Seb picked up her hand, turned it over and placed an open-mouthed kiss into the palm of her hand. Rowan shuddered and lust ran up and down her spine when he touched the tip of his tongue to her palm.

'Absolutely it's a threat,' Seb said, before attacking his burger.

Seb cast another look at Rowan as they walked down the steps to his car, parked by the front door earlier, and thought about walking into that cocktail party with her hand in his. Her dress would be enough to have the older men choking on their drinks, their wives raising an over-plucked eyebrow and any man below sixty sending approving looks at her stunning legs, from thigh to the two-inch silver heels she had absolutely no problem rocking.

She was gorgeous, with her wild hair pulled back into a casual roll, minimal make-up and a coral lipstick that perfectly matched the red of her dress. She looked fresh and sexy and he was already anticipating the end of the evening, when he could strip it off her as he'd promised. Which was insane, since they'd made love just over an hour ago and again this morning. And twice last night after they'd got back from visiting that antiques market, where Rowan had tried to persuade him to buy a silver cigarette case he didn't like and certainly didn't need.

'It's old and it's valuable. You could double your money,' he remembered her insisting.

'It might be old but it's ugly,' he'd replied, not telling her that he earned more money in fifteen minutes than he'd make on the hideous case.

He'd offended Rowan's horse-trader instincts for about a minute—until another pretty object had caught her attention and their brief argument had been totally forgotten as she'd engaged stallholder after stallholder in conversation.

It had taken them for ever to visit every stall—which

she'd had to do. She was so charming, easily drawing people into conversation and melting the sternest or shyest heart there. She had a natural warmth that just pulled people to her, he thought as he drove down the driveway.

'You look…God…amazing, Ro,' he said, turning left into the road.

'Thanks. You don't look too shabby yourself. I like that suit.'

Rowan placed her hand on his thigh and he could feel her warmth through the fabric of his black suit. He'd teamed it with a white shirt—no-brainer—but Rowan had swapped the tie he'd chosen—black—for a deep blue one he'd never worn in his life which, according to his sexy date, deepened the blue in his eyes.

He'd liked her choosing his tie… Seb sighed and reminded himself yet again to get a grip, catch a clue.

She. Was. Leaving.

As in bye-bye, birdy.

Next week.

And he was getting goofy because she was picking out his ties.

Get over yourself, already, Hollis.

Rowan's fingers dug into his thigh. 'Seb, stop!'

He slammed on the brakes. 'What? Jeez!' He looked past Rowan, down her parents' driveway, and saw Heidi and Stan standing in the driveway, pulling bags out of their sedate sedan.

'Oh, crap. Your parents are back.'

'Looks like it.' Rowan bit her lip and lifted her hand as her parents swivelled around to see who was idling at the bottom of their driveway. She turned and looked at Seb, her heart in her eyes. 'It would be so much easier if you just drove on.'

Seb touched her cheek with his thumb. 'I'm right behind you, babe.'

'Well, at least I'm looking my best,' Rowan quipped in a small voice as he turned off the engine.

'You look fantastic,' Seb said as he left the car, walked around and opened the passenger door for Rowan.

Heidi and Stan walked down the driveway to greet them.

'Seb, hello!' Heidi called as Seb took Rowan's icy hand in his. 'We're back—as you can see.'

'Stan…Heidi.' He placed his hand on Rowan's back and pushed her forward. 'So is Rowan.'

'Mum…hi, Dad.' Rowan stepped closer, reached up and brushed her father's cheek with her lips, leaned in for a small hug and then turned to her mum. Seb clenched his fist when Heidi pulled back and Rowan's lips brushed the air about two inches from her cheek. She couldn't even kiss her, hold her, after nine years apart?

What the…?

Who *was* this woman? Had he ever really known her? Had he been so blinded by the fact that she was there every day that he thought she was marvellous for that alone? No, he'd seen her interact with Peter—loving, kind, affectionate.

His heart clenched for Rowan as she stood back and straightened her shoulders. 'You're both looking well.'

'How long have you been home?' Her father took her hand, held it tight. 'It's so good to see you. You look beautiful—so grown-up.'

Rowan smiled. 'Seb and I are going to a party. I arrived about two weeks ago…I needed to come home unexpectedly. Seb's been helping me out.'

Heidi lifted her eyebrows and pursed her lips at Seb's hand, resting on her hip. 'Seems like he's been doing more than helping you out. Strange, since you could never stand each other before.'

Seb started to speak, but Rowan gripped the hand on her hip and he got the message. *Shut up, dude.*

'I've grown up, Mum.'

Heidi looked her up and down. 'Your skirts certainly haven't.'

'Mum! Nine years away and all you can do is gripe about my clothes?' Rowan snapped.

'Well, I think you look gorgeous, Ro.' Stan jumped into the conversational bloodbath. 'Absolutely terrific.'

'Well…' Heidi folded her arms. 'I'm tired, and you two are going to be late for wherever you are going. Maybe you should be on your way.'

'Heidi!' Stan protested, and Seb's temper simmered.

'We'll see her again,' Heidi said. 'Tomorrow. Maybe.'

Stan sent Rowan an apologetic look and Rowan stepped into his arms and gave him a longer hug. A hug Seb was pleased to see that he returned. He kissed her head before they stepped apart. 'I'll see you in the morning, Ro. It's good to have you back, darling.'

Rowan nodded and held onto Seb's hand with a death grip. 'See you then, Dad. And it's good to be back. Night, Mum.'

'Goodnight, Rowan. Sebastian.'

Seb pulled Rowan back to the car and opened the passenger door for her, helped her in. When he was back in his seat he placed his hand on the back of her neck. 'You okay, Ro?'

'Sure.' Rowan shrugged, her eyes on her parents, who were walking into their house. 'Situation normal. My mum cool and uninterested; my dad the buffer between the two of us.'

'She called me Sebastian. She's never called me that.'

Rowan managed a smile. 'It's because you're sleeping with me. She thinks you can do better.'

'Then she's an idiot.' Seb dropped his hand and started the engine. 'I need a drink. A couple of them.'

'Me too. Lead me into temptation, *Sebastian*.'

'Buzz off, Brat,' Seb shot back, but he kept his hand on her knee the whole way up the coast to the cocktail party.

In Seb's bedroom, much later that evening, Rowan slipped off her dangly silver earrings and dropped them onto Seb's credenza, next to his wallet and keys. 'Jeez, who would've thought I would run into Joe this evening at the cocktail party? I mean, heck, this is a big city. What were the chances?'

'Fairly good, I'd say, since he's reputed to be one of the most up-and-coming young businessmen in the city and it was a Chamber of Commerce function.'

'Up and coming dipstick, more like it,' Rowan muttered. 'Thanks, by the way.'

'For...?'

Seb shrugged off his jacket and Rowan could see the residual annoyance in his eyes. She knew that Seb had wanted to clock Joe, but he'd just cut him off at the knees with one burning look when he'd tried to engage them— her—in conversation.

'For sticking close...for not letting him near me.'

'My absolute pleasure,' Seb muttered, taking a step towards her. 'Why are we talking about him and why aren't you kissing me?'

'An epic fail on my part,' Rowan admitted, putting her hands on his waist.

'Damn straight,' Seb replied.

Rowan lifted her mouth to his, touching those surprisingly soft lips that could kiss her so tenderly but could also utter soft, deadly words that could strip hide. But he was only tender, only affectionate with her. He tasted of the whisky he'd sipped earlier, and as he opened his mouth to allow her to explore further she sensed a change in him.

This wasn't just about sex and pleasure any more, about maximising the moment. This kiss and the lovemaking that would follow were about making memories, capturing tastes and feelings that would sustain them when they separated.

Seb lifted his head and his deep, sombre eyes held hers as his hand travelled down the back of her neck to the zip of her dress. He pulled it down, one tantalising inch at a time, his fingers touching the skin beneath until the fabric gaped open to her buttocks. Using one finger, he pushed the fabric off one shoulder and then the other, until the dress fell in a frothy puddle over her feet.

Seb shoved his fingers in her hair and gently pulled the pins out, winding her curls around his hand before allowing the weight of her hair to fall down her back. Bending down in front of her, still fully dressed except for his jacket, he lifted one foot and deftly undid the ankle straps of her shoes. His fingers lightly caressed her ankles before he sat back on his heels and allowed his hands to drift up her calves, to explore the backs of her knees, the tops of her thighs.

'You are so beautiful,' Seb said, placing his forehead against her thigh.

Rowan frowned as she stroked his head. He sounded sad, she thought. Scared. As if this was just becoming a bit too much for him, a little too intense.

No, that was how *she* was feeling...

'Seb? Are you okay?'

'Fine,' Seb said, his words muffled.

He placed an open-mouthed kiss on her right knee and Rowan felt the familiar rush of heat, the tightening of her chest. How much longer would she feel like this? The intensity of their lovemaking couldn't last for ever—it never did. Then again, they didn't *have* for ever. They only had next week and then she would be gone. But she would enjoy every nerve-tightening second while she had the chance. She owed it to herself to do that.

Rowan stepped back, reached down and lifted Seb's tie, pulling it apart and allowing it to hang against his white shirt. Her fingers slipped between his neck and his collar and she snapped open the top button and then the next. Sinking to her knees, she placed her mouth on that masculine triangle at the bottom of his throat and inhaled deeply. God, she loved his smell.

Her fingers opened the rest of the buttons, and she shook her head when he tried to undo the clasp of her lacy bra.

'No, not yet,' she whispered. 'Let me play. I need to touch you, know you, taste you...'

'Why?' Seb demanded hoarsely.

Rowan bit her bottom lip as their eyes collided. 'So that I can remember every detail of you.'

'We could do this for a while yet, Ro. Nobody is making you go.'

Rowan shook her head as her hands slid over the bare skin of his sides. 'That's just sex talking, Seb. We both know that this can't last—won't last. You don't want a full-time lover and I can't stay in one place. We know this, Seb.'

'I just can't imagine not doing this any more,' Seb muttered, his face in her neck.

'Right now, I can't imagine going.'

Rowan pushed the shirt off his shoulders, stood up and pulled him to his feet. Small hands undid the snap of his suit pants and pushed the fabric off him, so that he stood naked in front of her, his erection hard and proud. Rowan ran her thumbnail down him and he jumped in reflex.

'Sit on the bed,' Rowan told him.

Rowan sat on the edge of his knees and her hands flowed over his broad shoulders, explored his tattoo and ran over the ridges of his stomach. 'I'm going to miss you when I go. I didn't think I would, but I know that I will. Lean back on your hands.'

Seb obeyed and tipped his head back. He stared at the

ceiling, his chest rising and falling rapidly. 'Don't just slip away without telling me,' he said, his voice vibrating. 'When you say goodbye, say goodbye. Don't sneak out.'

Like your mother did, Rowan thought. 'I promise. When I know I'm going, so will you. I promise to say goodbye properly.'

Rowan stroked her hand over his lower abdomen, moving her hand into his thatch of hair, down his penis and around to cup his balls. She felt him tense, relax, then groan.

'You're driving me crazy, Ro.'

Rowan was enjoying the power she was wielding, having this fantastically smart, sexy man under her control. It made her feel immensely potent to feel his reaction to her, to know that he was surrendering to her, trusting her to take care of him.

'I need to be inside you,' Seb groaned, launching himself upwards.

Rowan slipped off him and knelt in front of him, her fist encircling him, hard, warm, pulsing madly.

'Ro, don't. I won't be able to stop. I need you so much as it is,' Seb begged, his eyes wide in the dim light of the room. 'I won't be able to wait for you.'

'You can owe me...' Rowan smiled wickedly before her lips encircled him. She knew she'd won when his hand burrowed into her hair and his back bent over her head...

Was it so bad that she wanted him to keep a few erotic memories of her as well? Rowan certainly didn't think so.

CHAPTER TEN

'WELL, WELL, WELL...look what the cat has dragged in.'

Rowan thought she was still dreaming when she heard the gravelly voice—thought she was having a hallucination from too much sex and too little sleep when she saw Callie sitting at the dining table in the kitchen at Awelfor, blonde hair in a ponytail and her bare feet up on the corner of the table.

Callie?

'Callie!' Rowan screamed.

'Ro!' Callie shouted back as Rowan bounced forward and flung her arms around her best friend's neck, nearly toppling her off the chair.

Callie's arms wrapped around Rowan's back to return the hug, but when Callie's hand landed on her bottom Rowan lifted her eyebrows, then her head, and looked into Callie's green eyes.

'Are you copping a feel? Because if you are I have to tell you that you're not my type,' Rowan said, leaning her butt on the table, where Callie still had her feet.

'Just checking that you're wearing panties and haven't turned into a total slag while you've being bonking my brother.'

Callie grinned and Rowan's heart turned over. She and Seb shared that same smile—why had she never realised that until now?

'Coffee. I need coffee.' Rowan hoisted her bum off the table and wandered over to the coffee machine. She stared at it helplessly. 'Dammit, I hate this thing!'

As Rowan reached for the instant coffee she felt Callie shoulder her aside. 'Hasn't His Majesty shown you how it works?'

Rowan shrugged. 'He normally makes it for me himself; if he's not here I settle for instant.'

'It's not rocket science, BB.' Callie showed her what to do, and within a minute Rowan had made herself her first cappuccino.

'Awesome.' Rowan sipped and headed back for the table, sitting down before she started peppering Callie with questions. 'Why are you back? What happened to your Yank lover? Your appointments in LA and Vancouver?'

Callie quickly answered and then flipped the attention back to Rowan. Placing her face in her hands, she eyed her. 'You're glowing. I've never seen you glow.'

'Good sex.'

'I have good sex all the time and I never glow.' Callie's eyes radiated concern. 'What are you doing, Ro? Have you thought this through? Has Seb thought this through?'

Rowan sipped her coffee before sighing. 'I don't know... I can't speak for Seb—you know that he doesn't wear his heart on his sleeve. As for me... I went into this thinking it was just about sex, that I could control this...craziness I feel for him.'

'And can you? Did you? Have you?'

Rowan stared into her cup and wondered what to say. 'I have to, Cal. I can't do anything else but control it. I'm leaving. I have to leave.'

'Why?'

Rowan frowned at her. 'What?'

'Why do you have to leave? Who says that's the rule?

You've never been swayed by arguments about what one is "supposed" to do. So why do you now have to leave?'

Callie's verbal punch landed in her stomach. But if there was anyone she could be totally honest with it was Callie. 'Because staying is far too scary.'

'Why, sweetie?'

Rowan took a deep breath as her eyes filled with tears. 'Because I could love him, Cal. Really love him. But I don't know if I could love him enough to stay, to give up my freedom.'

'You'll never know if you don't try,' Callie pointed out.

'I'll never hurt him, or myself, if I leave before this takes on a life of its own,' Rowan said. 'I can leave now, but if this goes any deeper—if I fall in love with him—I'll be ripped apart when it ends. And it always ends, Cal.'

'Just don't leave without explaining to Seb exactly what you're doing,' Callie warned her, and Rowan remembered her promise to Seb the night before.

'I won't, Cal.' Rowan ran her finger around the rim of her cup and blew air into her cheeks. 'So that's where I am—emotionally, mentally. But I have no idea what Seb is thinking. He's probably not interested in anything more than what we have.'

'You guys really should talk more and bonk less,' Callie grumbled. 'Where *is* His Wonderfulness?'

'Still sleeping.' Rowan looked self-satisfied. 'I kind of wiped him out last night.'

'Blerch.' Callie shoved her fingers in her ears. 'Too much information.'

'Then I don't suppose you want to know about the lady kissing your dad on the cottage balcony at the moment?'

Callie slapped her hands over her eyes. 'No! What is *wrong* with you people?' She spread her fingers and looked at Rowan. 'Please tell me that she's older than us for a change.'

'A little older.' Rowan laughed. 'Okay, a lot older.'

Callie slowly lowered her hands. 'How much older? Five years? Ten?' she asked hopefully.

'Try thirty.' Rowan grinned.

Callie turned around and through the kitchen window looked at Annie, who was standing in Patch's arms and laughing up at him. In the morning sunlight they could see the fine lines around her eyes, the lack of tone in her arms. But her face was radiant and Patch's face reflected her happiness.

They looked like happy-ever-after.

'Oh, my, I think I'm going to cry,' Callie said, her words soaked with emotion. 'I think my daddy might be in love.'

'Crap on a stick,' Seb said from the doorway. 'That's all I need to hear. I'm going back to bed.'

Callie jumped up, snaked her arms around Seb's waist and squeezed. 'If I have to watch them play tonsil hockey so do you. Hey, big bro'.'

Seb dropped a kiss on her blonde head as he tucked her under his arm. His two favourite women in the room, and Ro was making him coffee. At least he hoped she was—though he thought that he needed it intravenously injected for the caffeine to have any effect soon.

Rowan walked to the fridge to grab a carton of milk and Seb had to hold Callie tighter to keep from reaching for her. Not necessarily to start anything—he was wiped!—but he just wanted to touch her, connect with her.

This was ridiculous, he thought. He'd never wanted to be close to someone before, had never sought out female company, yet he wanted to be closer to Rowan, needed to spend time with her outside the bedroom. He wanted more than sex. He needed...*time*, he decided. He just wanted more time.

Her parents were back and, judging by the looks she was sending towards their house, he could see that she was nervous about a repeat of last night's dismal performance. Seb stepped away from Callie and took the cup Rowan held out to him. He wanted to discuss her parents with her, see where she was mentally, and reassure her that he would go next door with her if she needed him to.

'Any chance of breakfast?' Callie asked brightly.

'Pancakes and bacon?' Rowan quickly responded with the suggestion of their favourite childhood meal—the only one that they could ever cook with any success.

'Whoop!' Callie bounced up again—Tigger on speed— and yanked open the freezer, looking for bacon.

'Top left?' Seb suggested, dropping into a chair and placing his bare feet up onto the seat next to him. *Coffee, kick in, please.*

He watched in resignation as Callie and Rowan fell into conversation as if they had seen each other yesterday, and tuned out automatically when they started discussing Callie's latest boyfriend in case he heard something he'd rather not...

Like the fact that Callie was having sex. Which he did not need to know. *Ever.*

Seb sighed into his coffee. He loved his sister, but he cursed her returning to Cape Town right now. He was selfish enough to want Rowan to himself for the little time she was in the country.

'Anyway, he was spectacular in the sack, but he couldn't hold a conversation with a stump.'

He saw the look Rowan sent his way, caught the teasing glint in her eyes because she knew how uncomfortable he felt hearing this stuff.

'Spectacular in the sack? Tell me more.'

'If you do, I'll beat you,' Seb interrupted, and changed the subject before they ganged up on him. 'Have you done any work on your netsukes, Ro? Anything?'

'Some.'

'Hallelujah.'

'There's no need to be snarky.' Rowan gently smacked the back of his head.

'You took two weeks to find out information I could probably have found in an hour. If that,' Seb retorted. 'I think snarky is called for.'

'I hate a bragger.' Rowan flicked his shoulder and Seb caught her finger and tugged her closer.

'That's not what you said last night,' Seb said, his voice silky as his brain started to fire on all cylinders.

Callie cracked an egg into a bowl and pulled a face. '*Eeew!* Gross! TMI, thank you. Tell me about these net-sukes so that I can push the thought of you two out of my head.'

Seb kissed Rowan's finger before letting her go.

Rowan wrinkled her nose as she opened the bacon. 'Well, they definitely aren't stolen. I found out that much. The four netsukes stolen from that gallery aren't anything like the ones I have, except for the subject matter.'

'Well, that's a relief.' Seb leaned back in his chair. 'So, what's the next step?'

Rowan pushed her hair behind her ears. 'I spoke to Grayson again, and he's scheduled a trip to London in ten days. If I can meet him in London he'll look at them and make me an offer.'

Seb fought to keep the dismay off his face and out of his voice. Ten days. She'd be out of his life in ten days. No, that didn't sound right.

Rowan carried on speaking and he forced himself to concentrate.

'I've some money to contribute to the airfare back to London, but—' she picked up a dishcloth and pulled it through her fingers in agitation '—I'd have to pay you the balance when I get to London, after Grayson has paid me. Is that okay with you?'

Seb managed to nod. Nothing was okay about this situation. Wanting to get closer to her, not wanting her to go, imagining her in his bed, in his life, for many more days, weeks—years, a lifetime... *Dammit!*

Seb watched her fry the bacon and thought it was deeply ironic that he'd been so on guard with his previous girlfriends, constantly batting off their attempts to get closer, and yet Rowan had pulled him in without making any effort at all.

He wanted to be with her and it was all self-imposed; he wanted to be with her, spend time with her, purely because he thought she was so damn wonderful. By not putting any pressure on him she'd untied the knots—the fear and concern over commitment—little by little by herself.

Was this what love felt like? He didn't think so. Who fell in love in two weeks? That was crazy! But he had had to admit that he was ass-deep in something. Something beyond lust, beyond attraction.

You just need some time alone to think this through, to be logical and practical, he insisted to himself. When she gave him some time to catch his breath he'd work it through, put the various components of what he was thinking into their proper boxes and he'd understand.

He needed to understand.

Seb tipped his head back and stared at the ceiling. She had to go. She would run because she needed to be free...

His heart wanted to flop at her feet and beg her to stay.

His brain told him he'd be okay—that things would go back to normal, that he'd plug the holes she'd made. Eventually. Maybe.

'Hey, you lovebirds! Stop snogging!'

Seb jumped at Callie's yell and saw his sister leaning across the sink, her face to the open window. 'You guys want pancakes? And, Dad, is she going be my new *mummee*?'

Rowan's eyes brimmed with mirth as she turned to look at him and his breath caught in his throat.

'Your sister—so shy, so bashful. She really should learn to put herself forward more.'

Rowan, her head reeling, carried the dinner dishes from the formal dining room to the kitchen and placed them on the counter for Seb to pack them into the dishwasher.

She'd had coffee with her father the morning after they'd returned home and then she'd waited two days for the invitation to dinner that her father had assured her was forthcoming. When it had never materialised, she'd bitten the bullet, called her dad and asked whether they'd like to have Sunday brunch with her and Seb.

It had been an unmitigated disaster.

Rowan felt Seb's arms around her waist, felt his solid frame against her chest, and the tears that she'd ruthlessly suppressed floated up her throat. 'I'm not sure whether to laugh or cry,' she said, her voice wobbly.

'At which part?' Seb asked, his lips just above her ear. 'There were many highlights. Your lack of a formal education, the fact that you are no better than a vagrant, your criminal past...'

'I'd heard all those before.' Rowan pushed her hair out of her eyes. 'What I *didn't* know was that they are putting the house on the market and moving to the UK to be closer to Peter when he goes there. I thought that Peter was planning to remain in Bahrain. Did you know that he was moving? He's your friend.'

Seb's arms dropped as she wiggled out of them. 'We don't talk that often, Ro. A bi-annual call to catch up—that's it. So, no, I didn't know about his move to the UK.'

'And his girlfriend? Did you know that she's six months pregnant?' Rowan heard the shrill demand in her voice and knew that she was not going to be unable to keep back the tide of emotion that was threatening to engulf her.

'No, I didn't know.'

Rowan moved a pile of plates from one stack to another, dumped the cutlery in an oven pan. 'Well, if that's not a huge bloody clue that they no longer consider me a part of this family then I don't know what is. I never thought it could still hurt this much.'

'What, Ro?'

'Knowing that I am, categorically, on my own,' Rowan whispered.

She'd always had this little dream—one she took out only occasionally and let it fly—that she was the beloved daughter, the fun sister, that she would have a relationship with her mother that was normal, loving…involved.

Well, their prosaic announcement earlier had detonated that fantasy into a million bloody shards. Every one of which was embedded in her heart.

'You're not on your own. You're part of us. You've always been part of us,' Seb stated, his voice calm and reasonable. Steady.

God, she wished she could climb into his steady and rest awhile. But she couldn't—wouldn't. Whatever they'd had was at an end. Her ties were cut with her parents and she should cut them with Seb as well. While she could.

They would be friends, would some day look back on the madness that had been their affair and smile, knowing that it had been a marvellous interlude in time that was pure fantasy.

'You are part of us,' Seb repeated.

Rowan shook her head. She wasn't—couldn't be. If she couldn't be accepted by her own family, how could she expect to be part of theirs? Especially after being away for so long. And what would that mean while she was on the road? The occasional call to Seb? To Patch? E-mails? Facebook?

It didn't work. She knew this.

Seb's hand drifted over her hair, a touch of pure comfort, and she jerked her head away. She had to start stepping back, start preparing herself to leave.

Practically she needed to get London to sell the netsukes, to bolster her bank account. To repay Seb.

Emotionally she had to pull away, to put some distance between them before he did. She couldn't bear it if he rejected her too—and he would. He'd made it very clear that what they had was a brief fling. He'd said nothing to make her believe that he wanted her to stay.

The realisation that a big part of her really wanted to stay terrified her.

'Oh, I took a call for you earlier, while you were in the shower,' Seb said, stepping away from her and leaning against the opposite kitchen counter.

'From..?'

'Melanie? Melissa?'

'Merle?'

'That's it. She said that you spoke to her the other day about organising her wedding?' Seb picked up an orange from the fruit basket and dug his fingers into the skin, pulling the peel away.

'She's Annie's niece and she wants a Moroccan-themed wedding. Since I've been to Morocco, Annie thought I could do it.' Rowan closed her eyes. 'I'd love to do it; I have all these ideas running through my head.'

'When is it?' Seb made a pile of peel on the dining room table.

'Three months' time.'

'So do it,' he suggested blandly.

Rowan blinked as she tried to process his words. Stay here for another three months? Was he insane? 'What are you suggesting?'

'Stay here with me. Do the wedding.' Seb pulled a segment from the orange and popped it into his mouth.

'Are you mad? That's the most illogical, impractical, stupid suggestion you have ever made!' Rowan's voice climbed with every decibel. 'I have to get to London to sell the netsukes!'

'Planes go both ways,' Seb pointed out in his cool, practical voice. 'Go to London. Come back.'

'I need to travel,—to keep moving, Sebastian. To be free!' Rowan shouted. 'I can't stay here.'

'Have I put a ring on your finger? Asked you to stay for ever? No. I've suggested that you stay for another three months, to do something you obviously want to do and obviously enjoy. I thought that you could stay here with me, which you seem to enjoy as well. Or am I wrong about that?'

'I thought that this was a fling...'

'And I thought you were good at change!' Seb snapped back. 'If you were anywhere else in the world would you stay?'

'Yes, but—'

'Then why can't you stay here? For a little while longer?'

'Because you haven't thought this out! Because you're feeling sorry for me, wanting to protect me, wanting to help me out of another jam! This is an impulsive offer that you are going to regret when you've thought it through and you'll wish that you'd never opened your big mouth. I don't want to be something you regret, Seb!'

'You wouldn't be.'

'Of course I would, Seb! I'm great for a fling but I'd drive you mad long-term. I can't stick to anything. I'll waft from job to job, get involved in one project and then go off at a tangent to explore something else. I'd pick up stray people and stray animals and bring them home. I'd fill your home with crazy objects that you'd hate and colourful fabrics that would hurt your eyes. I'd turn this place upside down! Drive you nuts.'

'Just leave the War Room alone.'

Rowan didn't hear him, so intent on listing every reason why she couldn't stay. 'And I'd feel hemmed-in, constrained. I'd feel frustrated and then I'd get bitchy—and then I'd start planning trips and then I'd get depressed because I'd know that I couldn't leave you like—'

'Like my mother did.'

Seb's eyes had hardened and Rowan swallowed. Dammit, why had she compared her leaving to his mother's? If he could survive that, it would be easy to wave *her* goodbye.

Just tell me that you love me, Rowan silently begged him, *that this is something more than just sex and I'll be prepared to take the risk. Tell me that I am important to you, that I mean...something. Throw me a bone here, Seb. Persuade me to stay.*

Seb didn't say a damn word.

Rowan scrubbed her hands over her face. 'I'm going to get some air. This is going nowhere.'

'Good idea. But while you're out there think of this.' Seb dropped the orange, placed sticky fingers and hands onto her face and held her head still while he ransacked her mouth.

Tongues clashed and collided—frustration and fury combined with lust and confusion. His hand on her butt pushed her into him, so that she could feel the long, solid, pulsing length of him against her stomach, and under her hands his heart thumped and rolled.

Seb yanked his mouth away from hers and looked at her with wild eyes. 'Yeah, think of that, Rowan. And then tell me you can just walk away from it.'

Rowan held her fingers to her lips, still tasting him there as he stormed out of the kitchen. She heard him thunder up the stairs and the door to his bedroom slam shut.

She would think about that—of course she would!—
but she knew that thousand-degree kisses and fantastic sex
wasn't enough long-term. Because falling in love with him
properly would kill her if he didn't feel anything more than
fierce attraction for her. She didn't know if she could pick
up the pieces of her life again when he told her that he was
tired of her, that it wasn't working, that he'd had enough.

She'd been the second best child, the not-up-to-par
daughter, and she wasn't prepared to be the almost-good-
enough-but-not-quite, good-for-the-short-term lover.

She wasn't prepared to play guessing games with her
heart.

CHAPTER ELEVEN

ROWAN, NOT KNOWING where else to go, slipped through the gate into her parents' garden and headed to the north-east corner, to the mini-orchard, overgrown and neglected. In this place, between the peach and apricot trees, she and Callie had played, out of sight of both houses. It was a place where they could pretend, talk, wish, dream. Well, Callie had talked and she had dreamt.

God, she wished Callie was here. Callie would help her sort through her confusion.

'Rowan?'

Rowan spun around and hastily brushed the tears off her face. Her mum stood in front of her, looking deeply uncomfortable. Rowan held up her hands in defeat. 'Mum. What now? Why are you here?'

'I saw you streaking across the lawn, knew where you were going.' Heidi ran her hand through her still-black hair. 'Your father just tore into me, said that I was cruel to you.'

Yeah. Well. Duh.

'He thought I'd told you about Peter, about selling, moving. He thinks that we correspond regularly.'

Rowan tipped her head. 'Why did you let him think that?'

Heidi shrugged. 'I wanted to avoid an argument. I don't like arguing, conflict, trouble.'

'And I was trouble from the day I was born,' Rowan said bitterly.

Heidi didn't argue and Rowan cursed as pain slashed through her.

'Just go, Mum. I can't deal with you now.'

'When you were so sick, when you nearly died, I thought I would die too.'

Heidi's voice cracked and Rowan thought that she'd never heard her mum's voice so saturated with emotion.

'I was so scared… I don't think I've ever prayed so hard and so much. I loved you with every fibre in my being and the thought of losing you was too much for me to bear.'

What the heck…?

'When you recovered I suppose I…I retreated from you. I vowed to protect you, but I didn't think I could go through that again so I pulled back.'

Heidi must have seen something on Rowan's face because her lips twisted.

'I'm not good with emotion like you are, Rowan. I can't embrace it. I'm steadier when it's at a distance, when I am in control. Peter didn't demand that from me. You did.'

'So you pushed me away?' Rowan said, her voice flat.

Heidi nodded. 'People like us—me, your father, Peter, even Seb—we're intellectuals. We are brain-based not feelings-based. You were *are*—all feelings. All the time. You need to touch, taste, experience.'

That was true, Rowan admitted.

Heidi nodded. 'I know you think I was cruel, encouraging you to go overseas, but I knew that you needed to. To taste, experience. Though I did think you'd come home in a year or two, settle down into a degree, get it out of your system.'

'Don't start,' Rowan warned her.

'I didn't think it would take you nine years to come home.' Heidi twisted her hands together. 'It's easier when you're not here. I can push the guilt away. But looking at you, so beautiful…'

'Mum.' Rowan placed her hand over her mouth.

Heidi straightened her shoulders and tossed her head. 'As for this…thing…with Seb…'

Oh, jeez, she really didn't want her mum commentating on her love-life. 'Mum, I don't feel like I want to hear—'

Heidi interrupted her. 'You need to leave. Because the two of you—'

Rowan growled in frustration. *Stop.* Maybe she did want to hear what she had to say. 'What, Mum?'

'The two of you spark off each other,' Heidi said, flustered. 'Anybody with half a brain can see that. But you're going to hurt each other. You are too different, worlds apart. It's not built for long-term… Love isn't enough.'

We're not in love, Rowan wanted to tell her. *Not quite. Not yet.*

Heidi kicked a branch at her foot. 'I suppose we'll have to get this area cleared if we want to sell.'

'Mum! We were talking about Seb and I! Tell me why you think we could never work.'

'Because you are too irrational, too impulsive for him to live with long-term, and his inability to be spontaneous would drive you mad. He wants someone steady and settled and you want someone exciting and unstructured. You'd kill each other.'

'So you don't believe in the theory that opposites attract? That love can conquer all?'

Heidi shook her head. 'It doesn't—not in real life. In books and in the movies, maybe, but this is your life—his life—and it's not a movie and it's not a book. Save yourselves the heartache, Rowan. I know you and I know Seb. This will blow up in your faces. You'll get hurt. And, believe it or not, I actually think you've been hurt enough.'

Rowan, reeling from having such an intense conversation with her mother, sucked in her breath. 'Why are you telling me this now?'

'Because I have failed you in so many ways, so many times. I should've tried to understand you better, loved you more, held you more. Drawn you closer instead of pushing you away. I failed you. But—' Heidi's voice cracked. 'But if I can save you some heartache, some pain, maybe you can start to forgive me. Maybe I can start to forgive myself.'

Heidi wrapped her arms around her middle and Rowan saw that her eyes were wet. She couldn't believe that her mother, who never cried, was crying over *her*.

She was nearly out of earshot when Rowan finally forced the word through her own tear-clogged throat. 'Mum?'

Heidi turned.

'I'm often in London. I have a house that I'm renovating there. Maybe we can meet, just you and I? Have tea, some time together. Maybe we can find a way back to each other?'

Heidi took a long time to answer and Rowan thought that she'd lost her. Again.

'I'd like that, Ro. I'd really like that.'

Rowan was relieved that Seb's bedroom was empty when she reached it. She immediately went to the spare room, dragged her backpack out of the cupboard and hauled it back to his room.

Somehow her clothes had found their way into his walk-in closet. Panties in his sock drawer, shorts next to his T-shirts. When had they migrated there? Who'd placed them there? Seb...? Seb had put the washing away. Hell, she'd been so busy bartending and arranging parties that she'd never got around to doing much laundry anyway. Seb had just done it quietly, with no fuss.

Shirts, shorts, jeans. Shoes? Red cowboy boots, trainers, pumps, flats. They all stood on the shelves in his shoe cupboard, along with her sparkly silver sandals. Rowan bit her lip as she traced the design on the front of one shoe; she loved these shoes but she wouldn't take them. Like the coral dress, like Seb, she had to leave them behind.

The box containing her netsukes sat on an open shelf above the shoes and Rowan stretched up and pulled it down. She lifted the lid and furiously unwrapped the little statues until she found the one she was looking for—the one of the Laughing Buddha with mischief in his eyes.

She wouldn't be selling this one—wouldn't take it with her. This was Seb's—her gift to him. She'd planned on keeping it herself but, like her, he'd fallen in love with it the first time he'd held it. It didn't matter that it was probably the oldest and most valuable of the collection. Nothing much mattered now. She placed it on the shelf next to a pile of his T-shirts, where she knew he would see it.

She was leaving and she had a new life to make. Her mum was right. They would eventually decimate each other. While she had the right to take chances with her own heart, she didn't have the right to play fast and loose with his. With anyone's. It was better to be on her own, responsible for only herself...

No risk of being hurt. Of hurting him.

'Running again, Brat?'

Rowan turned and looked at Seb, who had one shoulder plastered against the wall, his eyes shuttered.

'Packing.' Rowan kept her voice even. 'We both knew that I'd be leaving once I saw my folks.'

'Yeah, but neither of us thought that we'd be burning up the sheets a day later. That changes things, Rowan.'

'It's just sex, Seb. You can find it anywhere.'

Rowan yelped when Seb streaked across the room, gripped her arms and glared at her.

'It is not just sex! Get it?'

'Then what is it?' Rowan demanded. 'And let me go. You're hurting me.'

Tell me. Tell me that you need me to stay. Give me something to work with, to take a risk on.

Seb dropped his hands and then threw them up. 'It's something! I don't know what it is, exactly, but we'll never find out if you don't stop running!'

Something? Something wasn't enough. Not nearly enough.

'I'm leaving. I'm not running!' Rowan shouted. 'And I never said I'd stay! Besides, what would I be staying for? Another couple of months of sex? What do you want from me, Seb? Can you tell me?'

Seb raked his hand through his hair. 'No. Maybe. Not yet. I haven't thought it through.'

'You see, that's the essential difference between you and me. It has to make intellectual sense to you and it just has to feel right to me.' Rowan sat on the edge of the bed.

'Does it feel right for you to stay?' Seb asked quietly.

'Yes! But the problem is…'

'What?'

Rowan lifted pain-saturated eyes to his. 'This time I know that it's smart to leave. That, no matter how right it feels to stay, I have to listen to my brain. Because this time I can't trust my heart.'

'Why?'

'Because you'll break it. And I'll break yours. We have the ability to do that to each other,' Rowan said in a quiet, determined voice. 'If I walk—run—leave now, we can avoid that. You can't give me enough of what I need for me to consider staying. I don't want to hurt you, and God knows I don't want you to hurt me. Let me go, Seb, please. It's for the best. You know it is.'

'All I know—*feel*, dammit!—is that you are running as fast and as far away from me as possible. But I've never begged a woman for anything in my life and I'm not going to start now.'

Seb walked over to his desk, shoved the chair so hard that it skidded across the floor and bent over his computer. His fingers skipped over the keys and ten minutes later—the longest ten minutes of her life—he turned back to face her.

His face and voice were completely devoid of emotion. 'I've booked you on a flight to London, leaving tonight. I've ordered you a taxi. It will be here in an hour. I'm sure you won't mind spending the afternoon in the airport. It's what you do, isn't it?'

'Seb, I'm doing what I think is best for us,' Rowan protested, trying once more to get him to understand.

'And where does what I want, what I need, what I think is best, come into it? All I'm asking is for some time, Rowan! A slice of your time so that we can work out what we want to do. We've been together for nearly three weeks! We're adults. Adults don't make snap decisions about the rest of their lives, about whether they're going to get hurt or not. I want time with you—time that you seem to be able to give to mountains and monasteries, temples, sights and cities but not to me!' Seb roared. 'So, really, take your excuses about doing what is best for us and get the hell out of my life.'

Seb slammed the lid of his computer closed, sent her another fulminating, furious look and walked out of the room. Instead of slamming the door, as she knew he wanted to do, he closed it quietly. Its snick was the soundtrack to her heart cracking and snapping.

Crap; she was *so* screwed.

'You look awful, darling.' Grayson Darling looked at her across the table in the English tea room and then at an original artwork just beyond her head. 'Love that painting.'

'Gray, I've drunk the tea, eaten the scones…can we talk netsukes now?' Rowan demanded, in a thoroughly bad mood. Then again, she'd been in a bad mood since she'd left Cape Town two weeks ago and it was steadily getting worse. Having to spend two hours with Grayson, making small talk over high tea, was just making her feel even more cranky—which she hadn't believed was possible.

She needed to do this deal with Grayson; the money she'd made arranging those parties and bartending was almost finished and she was sick of sleeping on a friend's pull-out couch.

She needed money. Fast. She'd played this song to death; hopefully after today she wouldn't have to hear it again.

Grayson wiped his fingers on a snow-white cloth serviette and sighed dramatically as he pulled the box towards him. 'Where is the charming Rowan I enjoyed so much?'

Back in Cape Town, with her heart. With Seb. Seb… Her heart clenched. She missed him so much—missed her heart, which had remained behind with him. Without it she was just existing, just skating.

She didn't skate. She didn't exist. She *lived*. It was what she did. But no longer. Not any more. Not without Seb. She'd thought that she'd been so clever, leaving Cape Town before she fell in love with him. But love, she realised, didn't stop to count the miles between them and had snuck inside her anyway.

'Oh, Rowan, these are wonderful,' Grayson said, appreciation in every syllable as he lined up the netsukes between them. 'Fantastic composition, brilliant condition. But you're missing one… Where's the Laughing Buddha?'

'It's not for sale.'

'Of course it's for sale; it's the jewel of the collection.' Grayson looked at her in horror. 'It's the one I want.'

Seb's the one I want… Okay, stop being a complete drip, Dunn, and concentrate. 'Sorry, Grayson. I gave it away.'

Grayson closed his eyes and shook his head. 'Dear God, you are a basket case. Get it back.'

'It's gone. Move on. Make me an offer on these,' Rowan demanded, exhausted.

She watched as Grayson examined the netsukes again and allowed her mind to wander. She recognised the light of acquisition in his eyes and knew that within a day she'd be a couple of thousand pounds richer than she had been when she'd emptied her bank account a month ago. Good grief, had it only been a month? How could so much have happened in so short a time?

Forcing her mind away from the path it travelled far too frequently straight back to Seb, she tried to make plans on where to go from here. Back to Thailand or west to Canada? Or home to Cape Town.

Every cell in her body reacted when she thought of Cape Town. She didn't want to go anywhere else. She wanted to go home, to Seb.

Being deported and being broke had catapulted her into a situation where she'd had to slow down, move beyond the good-time surface and come face to face, heart to heart, with another person. With Seb. And she'd loved what she'd found. She'd resisted it, resisted love, with everything she had, and it was hard to admit that freedom didn't stand a chance against not having Seb in her life.

She loved him. Just loved him with every atom in her body. He was her freedom, the next world she had to discover, understand. He was what had been missing from her life, what she'd been searching for all over the world.

And he was right. She ran when she most needed to stand and fight.

'Fifty thousand and not a penny more for all of them,' Grayson said.

Rowan blinked, smiled and held out her hand. 'Deal. When can I have the money?'

Grayson looked horrified. 'Rowan, dammit, you are supposed to negotiate! Haven't I taught you *anything*?'

'I know you're low-balling me, Gray—' Well, she did now. 'But I don't have the time to argue with you. How much do you have on you?'

'Ten thousand. Okay, I'll give you sixty,' Grayson muttered. 'I'd feel like I was robbing you if you took less.'

Rowan held out her hand. 'I'll take the ten and you can transfer the balance into my account as per normal. Maybe by then you'll realise that you are still screwing me and up the offer again.'

Grayson sent the netsukes a greedy look before pulling out a money clip from his jacket pocket. 'It's entirely possible.'

Rowan took the cash from his hand, stood up and dropped a kiss on the balding crown of his head. 'Thanks. Enjoy.'

'If you ever want to sell the Laughing Buddha I'm your man.'

Rowan shook her head. 'I'll tell the new owner, but he won't sell it.'

'Gave it away…sacrilege.' Grayson gestured to the pile of food still on the table. 'Where are you shooting off to in such a hurry? We've hardly made a dent in the food.'

Rowan grinned at him. 'Home. I'm going home.'

Dusk was falling and it looked as if someone was randomly sprinkling lights over Scarborough as the sea darkened to cobalt and then to midnight-blue. It was Seb's favourite time of the day and, pre-Ro, he had often spent this half-hour at his desk, whisky in his hand, just watching the transition from night to day. With all the lights in his office off, his staff, who were still at their stations in the War Room, knew better than to disturb him.

Seb took a sip of his whisky, felt the burn and was grateful he could feel anything.

Since Rowan had left he'd felt numb. And that was when he wasn't feeling lost and sad and crap. He was feeling opposed to thinking and he didn't like it at all. This was why he didn't get emotionally involved; this was why he kept his distance.

He was a walking, talking cliché. Drinking too much, thinking too much, wishing too much. Finding things to do so that he didn't go to sleep, because she was there in his dreams and it hurt too damn much when he woke up, rolled over and realised—again—that she wasn't there.

He just hurt. Full-stop.

The lights flashed on overhead and he lifted his hand against the glare. 'What the...? Dad?'

'Drinking in the dark is a new low, even for you,' Patch said cheerfully, sitting in the chair on the opposite side of the desk. He gestured towards his half-full glass. 'Got another of those for your old man?'

Seb pushed the glass across the desk. 'Take this one. I'm going to hit the gym and try and work out my frustration.'

'Horny?' Patch joked, but his eyes were serious.

Seb couldn't find the energy to pretend. 'Just sad.'

'You do have it bad. Have *her* bad.' Patch sipped the whisky, put his ankle over his knee and looked at his son. 'I thought she'd be the one to get hurt, yet you are taking a pounding.'

'Yeah.' That summed it up.

'I'm going to marry Annie,' Patch said, and Seb's head snapped up.

He was wallowing and his father was getting married? What the—?

'She doesn't know, and I haven't said anything, but she's the one. I just want to be with her for ever. I know it in here.'

He thumped his heart. 'So do you, if you'd stop thinking so much and take a chance.'

Jeez, he'd tried. His father didn't know that he was the one who'd asked her to stay, to give them some time, so he briefly explained the situation.

Patch sent him a pitying look. 'So you asked her to stay... what did *that* mean?'

'Excuse me?'

'Did you tell her that you love her? That you want to be with her?' Patch demanded.

'No. I just asked her to stay, to give me time to think. I just wanted time to figure it out,' Seb protested.

'And if she'd given you that time and you'd decided that you didn't love her? What then? Where would she have been then?' Patch demanded. 'What reason did you give her to stay? Why would she stick around, running the risk of getting closer to you, when she knew she could get heart-slammed at the end of it?'

Seb dropped an F-bomb and his head. 'I didn't think about it like that.'

'What is the one thing Rowan has been looking for all her life, Seb?'

'Uh...'

'Love, acceptance, a place and a person she can belong to. How can somebody as smart as you not know this?'

He wasn't smart with people. He never had been.

'So, what are you going to do about it, Seb? Are you going to track her around the world like you do your mum? Never making contact and making yourself miserable? Or are you going to reach out and try and make this work?'

Seb felt the slap of Patch's words. 'What? Whoa, back up! Do you think I *should* contact my mum?'

Patch sighed. 'I think that you either have to or let her go. Callie and I, we're reconciled to the fact that she is out of our lives. We're over it—over her. You? Not so much. I think it would be healthier if you either had a relationship with her or if you cut ties completely. No man's land is no place to operate from. Same with Rowan. Either take a chance or let her go. Don't be half-assed about it.'

'Jeez, Dad. Why don't you just let it rip, huh?'

'I'm trying. Get Rowan back, Seb, or get a grip! Just, for all our sakes, stop moping!'

And that was his dad's verbal boot up the ass, Seb thought. He took a deep breath and ran his hand over his head. 'I don't know where she is. I presume she is still in London.'

Patch rolled his eyes. 'You've been tracking Laura since you were sixteen and you're telling me you don't know where Rowan is? That you can't find out where she is going? What do you do every day, Seb? Get on that bloody machine and found out!'

Seb grinned, jumped to his feet and headed for the computer across the room. Within minutes he'd plugged in the necessary code and the result flashed up on the screen.

Holy hell… Were his eyes playing cruel tricks on him?

He felt Patch at his elbow. 'What? What's the problem?'

Seb pointed to a line on the screen. 'Do you believe this? Am I seeing things?'

Patch's hand gripped his shaking shoulder to steady him. 'No, bud, I don't think that you are.'

Rowan cleared Customs and Immigration and stood in the middle of the arrivals hall, staring at the mobile in her hand. *Seb Hollis*, it said. *Seb Hollis. Dial me, dial me. Just push the green button.*

She'd thought that asking him for a favour all those weeks ago would be hard, but it was nothing—*nothing!*—compared to the terror she felt now.

Please love me. Please keep me.

Yeah, as if she was going to come right out and say that!

No, she'd figured this all out. She was going to be rational and unemotional; she'd say that they had something worth exploring, that she would stay if he wanted her to, give them time to work it out.

She would not be the gibberish-spewing, sobbing, crazy, wildly-in-love person she knew herself to be. She would be sensible if it killed her—which it probably would, if the terror didn't get her first.

What if he refused to come and get her? What if she had to bang down his door to see him? What if...?

She was driving herself over the edge. *Just dial the damn number!*

Seb took five rings to answer. 'Seb? It's me.'

'Rowan.'

Rowan heard the tension in his voice and felt her stomach swoop to her toes. Oh, this was much, much harder than anything she'd ever done before. *Courage, Dunn. This is your do-over, your second chance. You're going to regret not doing this, so do it!* 'I need a favour.'

'Another one?'

'It's the last one, I promise.'

'Uh huh.'

Before her vocal cords seized up she forced her words out. 'Can you come pick me up? I'm back and I'm at the airport. And I need to talk to you.'

'Yeah. Okay. Stay where you are. Sexy jeans, by the way,' he said, before abruptly disconnecting.

What the...? She was taking the biggest chance of her life and he was commenting on her jeans? How would he know what she was wearing anyway? How *could* he know...?

'Really sexy jeans. I like the way they hug your butt.'

Rowan spun around and there he was...large, solid, *there*...right in front of her. Dear Lord, he was there. Rowan lifted her fist to her mouth and bit her knuckle hard. The pain reassured her that he wasn't a figment of her imagination, that he was real.

So damn real. As real as the hand that now covered the side of her face.

'Breathe, Ro.'

Tears that she'd sworn weren't going to fall ran down her face. 'You're here.'

'I'll always be here, if you let me,' Seb told her, his eyes radiating emotion.

'How did you know…? How? My flight? I only decided yesterday to come back…to come home.' Ro gripped his shirt and hung on. As long as she held him he couldn't disappear on her. 'How?'

'I keep telling you that I could track you on the moon if I wanted to. When are you going to believe me?' Seb placed his hand on her hip and pulled her closer. 'Come here. I need to touch you—all of you.'

Rowan burrowed her face into his neck, inhaling his scent, trying to climb inside him. One strong hand held her head there, another wrapped around her lower back, pulling her as close as possible. They stood there for many minutes, just holding on.

Maybe, just maybe, he'd missed her as much as she'd missed him.

'Can I come home, Seb? Can I come back?' Rowan asked when she eventually lifted her head, forcing herself to meet his eyes.

Seb placed a gentle kiss on her mouth before pushing a curl behind her ear. He stroked the pad of his thumb across her cheekbone before dropping his hand back to her hip.

'You *are* home. You *are* back,' Seb replied. 'And, frankly, it's about bloody time.'

They didn't speak much on the way home, but Seb's hand on her knee reassured her that they would—that they would find a way to move forward. She placed her fingers on top of his and her heart turned over when he smiled at her. Was that love she saw in his eyes, on his face, or was she just imagining it?

She was probably just imagining it… Yes, he was happy that she was back, but there was no point in jumping to conclusions. She was just setting herself up for a fall. It was enough—it should be enough—to know that that she loved him, that she was home, that she had to take every day as it came and treasure the time she had with him.

She felt Seb's fingers widen under hers, stretch, and then he patted her knee. 'You were gripping my hand so hard I lost all feeling. Relax, Ro, we'll sort this out.'

'We will?'

Seb sent her his cocky grin. 'Damn straight. I'm not letting you go again without a fight.'

Rowan looked puzzled. 'I thought that *was* a fight.'

'That wasn't even close,' Seb assured her. 'Now, put your hand back on mine, try not to stop the blood, and relax. We're going to get home, have a glass of wine and talk it through. Like adults. In a reasonable, mature fashion…'

They had crazy monkey sex instead. On the stairs…

They walked into the house and Seb closed the front door behind him and dropped her rucksack to the floor. 'I'll take this upstairs later. Do you want a glass of wine?'

Rowan shook her head. She didn't want anything. She just wanted that mouth on hers, that skin under her hands, him inside her.

'Ro? Water? Juice? Food?'

Rowan shook her head again and Seb looked at her, puzzled. 'Okay. What *do* you want?'

'You. Just you. Right now. Right here,' Rowan whispered.

And, while she craved his touch, she didn't expect him

to immediately back her into the wall, his mouth covering hers and his hands everywhere. On her breasts, on her butt, her thighs, skimming her face, in her hair. It was as if he was rediscovering her, re-exploring her, touching her for the first time.

And she needed him to feed off her as she was feeding off him. She shoved her hands up and under his T-shirt, pulling it over his head so that she could touch his stomach without the barrier of cotton, run her hands over his chest, up his neck.

'Do you have any particular attachment to this shirt?' Seb demanded, his voice hoarse in her ear.

'Uh? What? No.'

'Good.' Seb grabbed each side of her shirt and ripped it open, scattering buttons over the floor. 'Much better,' he muttered, shoving the sleeves down her arms and letting it fall to the floor.

A finger hooked the cup of her bra away and his mouth covered her nipple as lust swirled and whirled, hot and fast.

Underneath love quivered and sighed, hoped and dreamt.

'I missed you so much,' Rowan said as he unhooked her bra and threw it over his shoulder.

'This place was like a morgue without you. Get those jeans off,' he muttered, his fingers busy pleasuring her breasts.

'Get yours off too,' Rowan retorted as she wiggled the fabric down her legs.

'For you? Any time.' Seb shucked his jeans along with his boxers and stared down at her, his heart in his eyes. 'You are so beautiful, Ro. I'm so glad you're home.'

'Me too.' Rowan sighed, placing her fingers on his cheek. 'Now, why don't you show me how glad you are by—?'

Seb's mouth cut off her words as one hand hoisted her thigh, his other hand pulled aside her panties and he thrust into her, hard and deep, filling her body, her mind and heart.

Seb. There was only Seb—would only be Seb.

'Ah, *now* I'm home,' Seb said into her mouth. 'You're my home, Ro. Only you.'

Later, after they'd made love again in his bed, Rowan sat on the love seat in the window of Seb's room and was thankful that he'd said that he needed to run downstairs for a minute.

She needed that minute. She needed more than a minute. To catch her breath, to allow her brain to catch up with her body.

She was trying to be brave, trying not to worry, but her brain was now in hyper-drive, red-lining with worry. Had nothing changed while she was away? Were they just going to fall back into what they'd had? When were they going to talk, work this out, as Seb had suggested in the car?

And what, exactly, did his 'working it out' entail?

Rowan released her bottom lip from between her teeth as Seb walked back into the room, carrying a large tray. His boxer shorts rode low on his hips and his 6 pack rippled as he walked over to her.

'Stop looking at me like that or you'll be back on that bed so fast your head will spin,' Seb said as he placed the tray on the cushions next to her.

'Promises, promises,' Rowan replied, and frowned when she looked down at the tray. A bottle of champagne she could understand, and the two glasses, but the set of keys that looked like a carbon copy of his house set and a keyless car remote had her puzzled. There was also a red jewellery box on the tray...

A jewellery box? Oh, dear God...

'You're not proposing, are you?' she asked, in a very high, very nervous voice.

Seb laughed. 'Not today.'

Phew!

'Then what's all this?' Rowan asked as Seb sat down, keeping the tray between them.

'We'll get to the box eventually, but first…it's time to work it out, Ro,' Seb said, popping the cork on the champagne and pouring her a glass.

He handed it over and poured his own glass.

'Why did you come home?' he asked her bluntly.

Rowan licked her lips. 'I missed you.'

'I missed you too. And…?'

Rowan stared at the bubbles in her glass. If she said these next words she could never take them back. They would be out there for ever…and she was okay with that.

'I love you. I do… I never expected to, never wanted to, but I do. So I thought I'd come home, tell you that and see how you feel about it.'

Seb just looked at her, his glass halfway to his mouth.

The moisture in Rowan's mouth dried up and she swirled some champagne around her tongue to get it to work. 'Feel free to give me a reaction, here, Hollis.'

'I feel pretty good about it. I thought I'd have to drag those words out of you with pliers but you've astounded me again.' Seb reached across the tray, kissed her gently and ran his thumb across her trembling bottom lip. 'I love you too, by the way. In every way possible and in lot of ways I thought were impossible.'

Ah… *Aaaahhhhh!* Rowan's shoulders fell down from her ears and her cheeks deepened. Relief, hot and strong, pulsed through her.

'Good to know… My mum says that we will destroy each other. That we are too different, diametrically opposed.' Rowan thought it was important to tell him that her mother rated their chances as less than nil.

'Your mother talks a lot of crap,' Seb said mildly, playing with her fingers as he sipped his champagne. 'We'll be fine. Yes, you'll turn my life upside down, but as long as you leave the War Room and my hackers alone you can do whatever you want. And if you go too crazy I'll pull you back in. In the same way, if I get too stuck in my head, you'll bully me out of it. We're good for each other precisely because we are so different.'

'I've been independent for so long and I'm worried that I'll get restless, feel hemmed-in.' Rowan also felt it was important to warn him. Maybe staying in one place would be enough for her, being with him would be enough, but there might come a day that she needed to fly, just to know that she could…

'I know.' Seb gestured to the tray. 'I've thought about that. So, first things first.' He held up the set of keys. 'Keys to your house—this house. I don't want to hear any more of this "your bedroom" and "your house" rubbish. This house is as much yours as it is mine. Replace the furniture, paint the walls—do whatever you want; just treat it as yours, okay?'

'It's not mine.'

'Rowan…!' Seb warned.

'Or yours, or Patch's. It's Yas's, as we all know. And whatever I do I'll have to put up with Yas yapping on about it, so I'll think long and hard before I go mad. You might not care, but she will.' Rowan took the keys and bounced them in her hand.

Seb grinned. 'All true, but I'll back you if comes down to a fight.' He lifted up the credit-card-type key. 'Keyless car key. We'll share the Quattro until I get you something else to drive.'

'You can't buy me a car!' Rowan squeaked. 'I have money. I can buy my own car. I sold the netsukes.'

'Thanks for mine, by the way. I love it. It's kept me from going insane these past couple of weeks.' Seb tossed the key card into her lap. 'Are we going to argue about money and stuff for the rest of our lives?'

'Are you going to love me that long?' Rowan asked, her hands on his knees.

'Planning on it.'

Seb picked up the jewellery box and tossed it from hand to hand. Rowan saw fear flash in his eyes.

'Giving you this is hard for me, but I know that it's necessary.'

Rowan frowned, took the box, flipped open the lid and saw that it was a credit card. He was giving her a credit card? What on earth...?

'There's enough money there to buy you ticket anywhere in the world, any time you want to go. Enough for you to book into any hotel you want to, buy what you want to. It has a heck of a limit in that it doesn't *have* a limit.'

'Seb. Why are you giving me a credit card? I don't understand.'

Seb licked his lips. 'It comes with a couple of conditions.'

'I'm listening.'

'I'll pay for everything, but you have to promise to say goodbye, to tell me that you're going. No walking out. And you can't use it after we've had a fight. You have to give us—me—a chance to work it out before you run.'

Tears tumbled. That was fair. God, that was so fair. She nodded furiously. 'Okay.'

'And you have to promise me that you'll always come back, because if you don't I swear I'll find you and drag you back home. I love you. It took me nine years to find you and I am not letting you go again.'

'Oh, Seb.' Rowan used the heels of her hands to swipe away her tears. It was such an enormous gift, such a demonstration of how well he knew her, how much he trusted her.

'Is that a deal, Brat?'

Rowan nodded. 'Deal.'

'Good. I told you we could work this out. Do you love me?'

'So much!'

'And I love you.' Seb's eyes brimmed with all the emotion he usually tried so hard to suppress. 'So explain to me—again—why you aren't over here, kissing me stupid?'

Rowan sighed as she moved into his arms. 'Another very epic fail on my part. Must try harder.'

* * * * *

Mills & Boon® Hardback

February 2014

ROMANCE

A Bargain with the Enemy	Carole Mortimer
A Secret Until Now	Kim Lawrence
Shamed in the Sands	Sharon Kendrick
Seduction Never Lies	Sara Craven
When Falcone's World Stops Turning	Abby Green
Securing the Greek's Legacy	Julia James
An Exquisite Challenge	Jennifer Hayward
A Debt Paid in Passion	Dani Collins
The Last Guy She Should Call	Joss Wood
No Time Like Mardi Gras	Kimberly Lang
Daring to Trust the Boss	Susan Meier
Rescued by the Millionaire	Cara Colter
Heiress on the Run	Sophie Pembroke
The Summer They Never Forgot	Kandy Shepherd
Trouble On Her Doorstep	Nina Harrington
Romance For Cynics	Nicola Marsh
Melting the Ice Queen's Heart	Amy Ruttan
Resisting Her Ex's Touch	Amber McKenzie

MEDICAL

Tempted by Dr Morales	Carol Marinelli
The Accidental Romeo	Carol Marinelli
The Honourable Army Doc	Emily Forbes
A Doctor to Remember	Joanna Neil

0114GEN STD HB